THE GENERAL PRACTICE

A year in the busy life of a GP is a frenetic combination of joy, comedy and tragedy. The doctor has an exhausting work schedule as he struggles to cope with a smallpox scare, the suicide of his partner, the poignant death of a lonely Holocaust survivor and the unexpected bonus arising from a fatal traffic accident. As the year comes to an end the GP has time to reflect on the heartache and joy that the past twelve months have brought him, his family and his patients.

THE GENERAL PRACTICE

THE GENERAL PRACTICE

by

Rosemary Friedman

Dales Large Print Books
Long Preston, North Yorkshire,
BD23 4ND, England.

British Library Cataloguing in Publication Data.

Friedman, Rosemary
    The general practice.

A catalogue record of this book is
available from the British Library

ISBN   978-1-84262-744-0 pbk

Dales Large Print is an imprint of Library Magna Books Ltd.

Printed and bound in Great Britain by
T.J. (International) Ltd., Cornwall, PL28 8RW

TO M.T.

WITH LOVE

One

With general practice, as with apples, there were good years and bad. The year that started with the smallpox outbreak and ended with an event so fantastic that newspaper reporters were queuing up our garden path for days was both. It was good financially, and morally, fruits of the hard work I had competently, I hope, carried out; it was good because I did not drop dead from the coronary thrombosis I anticipated daily; it was good because of the ultimate and totally unexpected reward with which it left us, against which we would have laid odds at a million to one. It was bad because in its first six weeks no meal endured more than three and a half minutes; bad because I lost my partner in the most extraordinary circumstances; bad because at the end of it I was a shadow of my former self and had almost to be reintroduced to my wife and children. On looking back it was surprising almost that we had weathered it.

All in all it was a year.

It started very small.

Christmas had been quiet. No snow and not too cold and the customary welcome number of bottles on our sideboard together with a pair of malformed socks knitted with love by an old lady of ninety and some lemon silk pyjamas from Hong Kong.

The usual assortment of relations had come to stay and eaten too much Christmas pudding and hammered their fingers instead of the holly and well and truly taken to the Yuletide spirit and quietly gone again leaving their hosts, my patients, clearing the mess and muttering never again, 'Next year we'll have Christmas on our own.'

New Year's Eve was on Saturday and the following day was not my Sunday on duty so I was able to stay in bed from which, had the entire practice been perforating ulcers, I don't think I could have risen voluntarily.

'My God,' I said to Sylvia. 'I'm really ill. Nip down to my surgery and bring me the *Encyclopaedia of Medical Practice.*'

'Twenty-six vols?'

'Look up tumour. Cerebral tumour. And you'd better bring a bowl. And draw the curtains. And tell the kids to be quiet. And Sylvia, I really ought to make a will'

She was gone. I wondered if she'd get married again and if it would be to a doctor. Probably had enough, poor girl. I wondered what he'd look like and if she'd ever spare a thought for me.

She came back with a bowl and a bottle of Coca-Cola.

'Where's the encyclopaedia?'

'You don't need an encyclopaedia to diagnose a hangover.'

'Don't be facetious.'

'I'm not. What was her name?'

'Whose?'

'The anaesthetist whose eyes you were plumbing for three and a quarter hours.'

I remembered, through a cloud darkly, a party.

'Blonde?'

'Black roots. I doubt if she's feeling terribly healthy this morning. Drink this; slowly.'

I raised my head and a thousand crowbars attacked me over the eyes.

'You'd better bring that book; and tell Robin.'

'I've no intention of disturbing his Sunday.'

'He'll want to know I shan't be doing the surgery tomorrow.'

'You'll be doing the surgery tomorrow. Take another sip.'

'I can't. I'll be sick.'

'You'll be sick if you don't.'

'Of course it may be operable. A fairly large percentage of them are.'

Sylvia snorted. 'It's quite enough to have to drive you home, put you to bed and nurse you without having to listen to all this melodrama about cerebral tumours. You've a plain, ordinary, common or garden hangover which is just what you deserve and you can lie there and get over it while I go and see to lunch.'

'Don't bother to prepare anything for me. I wonder if Newton is better or Hackforth-Smith. I don't know all that many neuro-surgeons. Newton is better on the theory but Hackforth-Smith has such a superb technique. I think on the whole, perhaps Hackford-Smith.'

Sylvia was tying on a clean apron.

'They'll have to shave my head.'

'What's that?'

'My head. They'll have to shave it.'

'Why? Have you been fraternising with the enemy?'

'You'll be laughing the other side of your face ... oh! my head.'

'You see. Don't talk.'

'I can't. I can't even move.'

'Just think of that poor blonde.'

'I can't even do that. I must be ill.'

'I'm going to cook the chicken; *A la Véronique* with a *paillasson* of potatoes, followed by *Gâteau Ganache*.'

I hadn't the strength to throw anything. Anyway she was gone.

Sylvia, trained before our marriage for modelling, had been an erratic cook swinging from hamburgers nightly to such monstrosities as 'peas in lemon cases' extorted with pain from the highly coloured glossies.

For the past month however she had been attending an advanced and exotic French cookery course and was attacking it with all the vast enthusiasm of which she was sporadically capable.

On Tuesdays and Fridays she staggered home exhausted and shiny-faced carrying in triumph cardboard boxes from which she would produce with pride anything from a *potage bonne femme* to a *scallops St Jacques Chapon-Fin* or *salambos à l'orange* which represented our dinner. On Mondays, Wednesdays, and Thursdays it was back to the hamburgers. At the weekends, when there was more time, she experimented with the dishes she had learned. All in all, meals were definitely looking up.

I tried to think of other things, one burning eye upon the enamel bowl Sylvia had left next to the bed.

'Hand, foot and mouth disease,' I thought. A vision of *the crêpes au fromages* we had had last Tuesday drifted before me. 'Renal function in hydronephrosis.' Pear *vinaigrette* with cheese *sablés*.

I groaned. I was dying for sure. The symptoms were too severe for the tumour to be either benign or slow-growing.

The door opened. Penny, in trousers and sweater, came in and tripped over the enamel bowl.

Hot knives seared through my head as she

extricated herself.

'Why don't you look where you're going?'

'I've got my eyes closed.'

'What on earth for?'

'My holiday essay. "I am a blind girl".'
Head erect she trod round the room, her
arms stretched before her.

She bumped into the bed.

'Penny!'

'Sorry. I can't see.'

'Didn't Mummy tell you I was ill?'

'She said you had too much to drink last
night.' She fingered the objects on the dressing-table and put them down again noisily.

'Was it a nice party?'

'Not bad.'

'What did you do?'

'I don't know. Dance.'

'Do you like dancing?' She knocked over a
bottle of Sylvia's scent.

'It's all right.'

'Can I go to a dance?'

'You can go anywhere you like. But leave
me alone; please!'

'I'd hate to be blind.'

She walked into the door.

'Milton was blind.'

She felt for the handle.

'Did you know?'

'What?'

'Milton was blind?'

'You wait till you're ill.'

16

'Mummy says you're not ill. Anyway I wouldn't mind if I got Coca-Cola.'

She opened the door.

I tensed myself, waiting for the bang.

It took her a full minute to close it with less noise than a breath of wind. She released the handle with a clatter.

At seven-thirty next morning I felt fit but weak. Sylvia enquired tenderly after the tumour.

'I shall never treat a hangover,' I said regarding my pallid face in the mirror, 'with anything but the greatest sympathy. It is sheer hell.'

'Particularly for the relatives,' Sylvia said. 'Telephone!'

'Answer it, darling.'

I continued to remove my two-day beard.

'It's Mrs Francis. She wants to be vaccinated. So does her husband and the boys.'

'At this hour?'

'They'll come to morning surgery if you have the vaccine.'

'I suppose they're going abroad. All right. Tell them to come early.'

Robin arrived at eight-thirty, grey-faced.

'Happy New Year,' I said.

He grunted, unsmiling. He was customarily the most affable of partners.

Refusing coffee he sat next to me while I had mine and we went through the letters together.

Mr Low's X-ray revealed a shadow on his lung. Mrs Gibbon was recovering after partial gastrectomy and vagotomy. The result of Miss Menzies' IVP was normal.

'The Thomases are coming "en masse" for vaccination,' Robin said. 'Any vaccine?'

'Just about everyone seems to be going to far-away places. What's the matter with you this morning?'

'You're very lucky I'm here at all,' Robin said. 'I was extremely ill yesterday. I thought I was developing acute infective hepatitis.'

'Where were you on Saturday night?'

'At the Brookways'. They had a party at their house by the river.'

'Acute infective hepatitis you say?'

'I thought at one moment I was dying. I very nearly rang you.'

'I was pretty seedy myself.'

'What was it?'

'I'm not sure; pain in the frontal region, and double vision.'

'You don't look too good.'

'You don't look too good yourself.'

The telephone rang and Robin grunted into the receiver then scribbled an illegible note on *The Times*.

I squinted at it. 'Smith Junior hurt arm playing Ludo!'

'Judo!' Robin growled. 'Stop trying to be funny.'

18

Miss Nisbet, the baby-faced blonde who had been our secretary since leaving school, had got married a fortnight before Christmas.

'Well,' I said heartily as I handed her the morning's letters to file when she had dealt with the backlog of some hundreds of others which had accumulated while she had been honeymooning in Jersey, 'how's married life?'

She clapped a wedding-ringed hand to her head. 'Please don't shout, Doctor.'

'Not you too,' I said. 'Where were you on Saturday?'

'Party,' she whispered. 'Welcome home.'

Whispering soft, painful messages to each other through the intercom Robin, Miss Nisbet and I dealt with a quieter than usual Monday. The patients for the most part were in good form. Most of them wished me a Happy New Year; a few insisted on shaking my hand, callisthenics I could have well done without; Mr Whitfield, always the life and soul of the party, came in with bags under his eyes and asked facetiously for a death certificate.

'Where's your Medical Record Envelope?'

Miss Nisbet was supposed to hand them to the patients as they came in to the consulting-room.

'She didn't give it to me.'

I made a New Year resolution not to tolerate slackness and buzzed Miss Nisbet.

'Mr Whitfield's MRE!'

'I did ask you not to shout, Doctor.' Her baby-face belied her.

'Well where is it?' I whispered menacingly.

'I'm sorry, Doctor, I couldn't get it out.'

'Why not?'

'There's a spider in the "W"s.'

I vaccinated the Francises and the Thomases and coped as silently as possible with the rest of the New Year complaints. Miss Chalker who had been cruising in the Canary Isles at Christmas and who kept me supplied with socks and handkerchiefs came in with a parcel.

It was a tie, mustard wool, and would do well for Sundays.

'With your green checked shirt,' Miss Chalker said. She should know. She had bought it.

There were not many visits. When I asked Miss Nisbet for them she said, 'Mrs Bottomley.'

I wrote it down in the visits book. 'A new patient? What address?'

'That's me. Mrs Bottomley.'

'Well, what's the matter with you?'

'There's nothing the matter with me.'

'Then what have I written you on my visiting list for?'

'It's not a visit. It's my name.'

'Look, Miss Nisbet, please. I'm not in the mood...'

'Mrs Bottomley, Doctor.'

The penny dropped.

'Look, Miss Nisbet, I mean Mrs Bottomley, it's a lovely name, I mean it really is a lovely name, isn't it, Robin?' – Robin was sitting at his desk with his eyes closed and an expression of agony on his face – 'but couldn't we just go on calling you Miss Nisbet? It's so much, er, well shorter. Isn't it, Robin?'

He opened his eyes. 'Oh much. Much, much.'

'That's settled then?'

Miss Nisbet hesitated. 'I don't know what Ronald will say.'

'Well let's keep it just between ourselves,' I said. 'Just the three of us.'

'We three,' Robin said swigging from a bottle of Vitamin B syrup the traveller had left.

'All right then,' Miss Nisbet said.

I put an arm round her plump little shoulders. 'That's my girl.'

'Well just remember I'm a married woman.'

There was a New Year lull in the air. It wasn't cold and not many people about.

There were three visits on the Council estate. I parked in Shakespeare Close behind the dustcart which was blocking the road and walked towards number twelve. A grubby child came running from the end of the street. I presumed she was looking out for me and it was another visit. It was no one I recognised. She arrived breathless.

'What is it?' I said. Perhaps an emergency. She held her chest, puffed with running.

'Mam says, can she 'ave a sack o' coal!'

In the afternoon I slept.

'There's something ominous about this,' I said to Sylvia. 'We haven't had a Monday like this in years.'

'Just the New Year lull. What's all this about Penny going to a dance?'

'First I've heard of it.'

'Ooh, Daddy. You're promised.'

'I've never even heard about it.'

'I told you yesterday when you were in bed. You said I could go.'

'A dance! Don't be ridiculous. How old are you?'

'Eleven. The same as Peter. We're twins, remember?'

'There's no need to be cheeky. Where is it?'

'At the Youth Club. It's for tens to fifteens. With a proper band.'

'Whom would you dance with?'

'Boys. Roger Hill is going and Dennis Weatherhead.'

'Out of the question. You get on with your schoolwork.'

'It's on Saturday night.'

'When I was your age...'

She turned her eyes up. 'Please?'

'No.'

'Daddy...'

'I have to get washed; it's Surgery time.'

'Well can I?'

'No. Don't ask again.'

At the door she said histrionically: 'You're ruining my whole life!'

Mrs Tenby brought her children to be vaccinated; so did Mrs Graham. By the time Michael Post came in with rolled sleeves I had no more vaccine.

'It's odd,' I said to Sylvia over the hamburgers, 'Everyone seems to want vaccinations all of a sudden.'

Sylvia held up the evening newspaper. There was a two-inch headline.

SMALLPOX OUTBREAK IN LIVERPOOL. SIX NEW CASES SUSPECTED.

Two

In the queue at the public health laboratory for the smallpox vaccine I met Phoebe Miller, a neighbouring lady practitioner, Doctors Letts, Maugham and Talbot, who were members of our Sunday rota, and Doctors Green, Colgate and Weatherhead who were not.

'They're rationing it,' Phoebe Miller said. 'It's caught them on the hop.'

'Naturally; just to add to our difficulties.'

'I'm glad I met you anyway. I want to ask a small favour.'

'Of course.' I liked Phoebe Miller and she had often helped me out in the past.

'There's a dog show in Leicester tomorrow. Do you think you could cope with my little lot?'

'With pleasure.'

'It's terribly kind of you. Things are very quiet just now so I thought I may as well pop along.'

'Think nothing of it.'

'Twenty-five doses!' Dr Colgate said, coming back from the window with a small box and a stack of yellow cards. 'May be some more this afternoon.'

'I'll tell you what,' Phoebe Miller said. 'I'll

24

come back later and collect your second lot for you.'

'I'd be very grateful.'

'One good turn and all that...'

They had started ringing at seven that morning. 'This smallpox outbreak, Doctor, do you think my children should be re-vaccinated?' 'I'd like to be vaccinated, Doctor. May I come along to the surgery?' 'My husband has a jig-grinder in his factory whose brother-in-law shook hands with a man whose aunt comes from Liverpool. Do you think...?' 'I have to go to Southport on business, I wonder whether you could find time to...'

My twenty-five doses were not going to go very far.

When I got back Robin was on the steps. 'Where the hell have you been? I've got them standing round the walls.'

I explained about the twenty-five doses.

We vaccinated the first twenty-five patients and asked the others to come back in the evening having enquired first if we had any more vaccine. In her cubby-hole off the waiting-room Miss Nisbet was tearing her hair. 'Yes, Doctor is doing vaccinations but we haven't any more vaccine at present.' 'I don't think it will be possible before tomorrow.' 'Yes, if you're worried about it Doctor will vaccinate your "au pair".' 'No, I'm afraid he can't be done immediately. We haven't the vaccine. I'm sorry, we can't get it by five o'clock ... the Public Health Laboratory...' 'There may be some by tomorrow evening...' 'Try tomorrow...'

Everyone had gone mad. One mother panicked and the whole road rolled their sleeves and ran.

We started to fill in the yellow cards which informed the Public Health Department of each vaccination we performed and for each of which we would in time receive a fee of two-and-sixpence.

At three o'clock Phoebe Miller arrived with another very small package.

'Another twenty-five and that's all I could squeeze. I suggest you go yourself in the morning and make love to the redhead who's dishing it out. I have a suspicion Dr Talbot was giving her some of the blarney. How are things going?'

'Hopeless. The telephone hasn't stopped. Poor Sylvia is rushed off her feet. Yours is the same I suppose.'

'Couldn't say,' Phoebe said cheerfully. 'I go out and leave it.'

Phoebe Miller had a small practice, largely women and old people, and she did not depend upon it for her livelihood. We could not all go out and leave our telephones to ring.

Her two sealyhams and one golden retriever were yapping from the back of her battered Singer.

'Won't you come in for a bit?'

'Not likely. We're going for our afternoon walkies.'

'Thanks anyway for the "fix".'

She went back to her dogs and I to the telephone.

Some of them took an age to spit it out. 'This is Mrs Waterhouse, Doctor. I'm frightfully sorry to bother you, you know I'm not one of those, but I was just listening to the news on the BBC and they said there had been some sort of smallpox outbreak in Liverpool. I had the children vaccinated when they were little but I can't remember about Terence; he was having that trouble with his ears at the time if you remember and everything else rather went by the board. Anyway what I was wondering was whether you thought it advisable for them to be re-vaccinated, or rather vaccinated in the case of Terence. The only trouble is when we're going to fit it in. Sandra goes to dancing on Tuesdays and Thursdays and Michael has Cubs and extra coaching and of course Terence is now beginning to get busy with his GCE. They work them so frightfully hard these days, they really don't get a single moment to themselves. Firstly, what do you think about it all? Is it advisable for us to be done?'

I had decided to allow the patients to make up their own minds in this matter. The outbreak was at present small and quite far away. With vaccinations there was always a risk, however small, of complications.

I pointed this out to Mrs Waterhouse.

'Have you done your own children?'

'I haven't, no.'

'Well, I do think just to be on the safe side...'

'Fine, bring them along tomorrow night.'

'But it's Sandra's dancing. I thought perhaps tonight, and Michael could come along after Cubs if you don't mind if he was just the teeniest bit after seven-thirty...'

'There's no more vaccine for tonight. You'll have to bring them along tomorrow evening and take a chance.'

'But Sandra's dancing...'

'I'm sorry, Mrs Waterhouse, I'm frightfully busy... See you tomorrow night.'

I replaced the receiver. The telephone rang again immediately.

'Yes?'

'Holly Park 8099?'

'Yes.'

'This is the Operator speakin', we've had a "verify engaged" on your line. I'm puttin' the caller through now.'

'Hallo. Holly Park 8099?'

'Yes.'

'Is that the doctor?'

'Yes.'

'Well I'm sorry to trouble you, Doctor,

I've been trying to get you all day. There's something been worrying me a little bit. You see my mother-in-law lives in Liverpool, and she's just sent the kiddies a fire engine and a teddy-bear, a life-size one that is, for Linda for Christmas. What I was wondering was, if you've a moment to advise me on this, Doctor, is about this smallpox business. The kiddies were done when they were little of course, but Len and me, you hear so many stories...'

By the time the evening surgery started I was hoarse and irritable and Sylvia in a similar state from answering the telephone.

This time there was a queue down the garden path.

'It's useless more than twenty-five of you waiting for vaccination,' I announced, 'we've only that many doses. I'm hoping to get some more in the morning.'

Not a soul stirred.

'Well stand there if you like. I can only do twenty-five.'

We were answering queries until midnight.

At bed-time I said to Sylvia, 'If anyone rings in the night you answer it. Try to sort it out, there's a good girl, or I shan't be fit for the morning.'

We slept until half-past three when Sylvia lunged for the ringing telephone, missed, knocked over the glass of water on the bed-side table and hurled the lamp onto the floor.

'Hallo,' she said finally and listened. 'No, I'm sorry, Doctor's out.'

'Who is it?' I hissed. 'I didn't tell you to say I was out.'

'I'm protecting you,' Sylvia hissed back. 'It's Mrs Phipps. Her husband has a sore throat.'

'Tell him to take two aspirins and ring in the morning if he isn't better.'

Sylvia repeated the message to Mrs Phipps. She put her hand over the receiver again.

'She says he's already taken two aspirins.'

'Tell her to give him a hot drink.'

She passed on the instructions.

'He's already had a hot drink.'

'Tell him to make the room warm and go to sleep.'

Sylvia told Mrs Phipps, then listened for a long while.

'What did she say?' I hissed.

'She said, "Excuse me, but if that man in bed with you is a doctor perhaps he'd come and see my husband!"'

The next morning the nightmare started in earnest. Outside the surgery by eight o'clock it looked like the queue for the one-and-nines.

I managed to get a hundred doses of vaccine and a stack of yellow forms which I optimistically hoped would last me over the scare. Ours was a district of young married couples and I suppose the panic was worse

30

because mothers were afraid for their children.

It was ten o'clock by the time I got home with the vaccine. Outside the house the queue was now well round the corner; inside, things were even worse. The waiting-room was so congested that Miss Nisbet was incarcerated in her cubby-hole; the atmosphere, she informed me on the intercom was, to put it mildly, overpowering.

I set to work. By eleven o'clock, when I should have been starting the visits, I had vaccinated some thirty people and was tiring. By twelve o'clock we had reduced the queue to the garden gate. At five-past twelve Miss Nisbet buzzed, her voice tense with hysteria, to say Mrs Upjohn had fainted in the waiting-room.

'You'd better bring her in,' I said.

'I can't,' Miss Nisbet shrieked. 'I can't get through!'

I opened my door and Mr Hargreaves from the off-licence, fourteen stone of him, fell into my arms.

'Sorry, Doc. Bit of a pandemonium!'

Pandemonium was right. The people inside, some of whom, like Mrs Upjohn, beginning to be overcome by the heat were trying to get out. The crowd on the steps were pushing to get in. Mrs Upjohn had passed clean out but had no room to fall down. With the help of young Mike Rafferty who was a weight-lifter in his spare time and who lifted her up as if she were a dumb-bell I managed to get her into the surgery where I revived her, vaccinated her and helped her out through the window.

Mrs Buchanan was next.

'Roll your sleeve,' I said wearily, selecting a vial of vaccine.

She looked a little apprehensively but did as she was told.

I came round the desk with my needle.

'What are you doing, Doctor?'

'There's nothing to worry about. Just a scratch. It's not like an injection.'

Mrs Buchanan's eyes widened. 'But I only came for my sleeping pills.'

The vaccine ran out again before the patients. It was one o'clock and we still hadn't done any visits.

'That's the lot for this morning!'

They refused to budge.

'I can't do any more. I haven't any more vaccine. You'll have to come back tomorrow.'

'Can't I come back tonight, Doc?' Bert Wilcox, a long-distance lorry driver, said, 'I'm on the road termorrer. I might even 'ave to go to Liverpool.'

'I'll tell you what, Bert,' I said. 'You go and get some more vaccine for me from the Public Health Lab this afternoon, and you shall be the first this evening. I'll give you a letter.'

We got them moving. Miss Nisbet looked

as if she had been pulled through a hedge backwards.

'How many visits?' I said.

'Eight, and two for Dr Miller.'

I had forgotten that I'd promised Phoebe rashly for today.

'May I ask you something?' Miss Nisbet said.

'If it doesn't take more than two and a half seconds,' I said.

'Will you vaccinate me?'

I laughed tinnily.

'I mean it.'

'She's right,' Robin said. 'I mean look at all the people we come into contact with. We need it if anyone does.'

'Perhaps you're right,' I said. 'Anyway, we haven't any vaccine.'

'We'll do it with the next lot,' Robin said. 'You do me and I'll do you and we'll both do Miss Nisbet. We'll have a little party. Are you doing the kids?'

'Peter and Penny? Not at the moment. I think it's a lot of panic for nothing.'

In the High Street the newspaper placards did little to confirm my view. 'Two further smallpox suspects!' – 'Doctors call for more vaccine!' – 'Public Functions cancelled in Liverpool!'

At two-thirty I remembered I hadn't yet had lunch. There was one more visit for Phoebe Miller. I thought, with my last ounce of strength which sadly needed revictualling, I might as well polish it off.

It was above a row of shops. I walked past the baker's, the grocer's, the butcher's and the hardware store looking for the entrance to the flats with which I was unfamiliar. The woman in the hardware store directed me back past the butcher's, the grocer's and the baker's.

An old lady, confined to her room with Parkinson's disease, smiled at me sweetly.

'Where's Dr Phoebe?'

'She's having a day off. I'm doing her work.'

'Never mind, dear. It's always nice to see a new face. Did you bring the sugar?'

'The sugar?' I stopped in the midst of opening my case.

'Dr Phoebe always brings me a pound of gran. on a Tuesday. Never mind though, if you pop down Mrs Griggs will give it to you, she knows I can't get out, and a packet of Rich Tea if it's not too much trouble.'

I remembered about Phoebe Miller and her old ladies. No wonder they adored her. I got the sugar and the biscuits. I also posted a letter to the old lady's sister in Rhodesia and asked the oil man to deliver as soon as possible.

I then went home for lunch.

Bert Wilcox was on the surgery steps. He held a package aloft. I took it from him.

'Well done, Bert. Very kind of you. Thank very much.'

He didn't move.

'Can I come in and wait, Doc?'

'What for?'

'Me vaccination.'

'I can't do you before tonight. I haven't had any lunch yet.'

'If I come in now I'll be the first, see.'

'All right. I suppose so.'

Sylvia was answering the telephone: 'Bring him round this evening and Doctor will vaccinate him,' she was saying. 'Yes, bring him just before six and he'll be the first.'

I laughed hollowly. 'For your information the evening surgery has already started.'

By four o'clock the waiting-room was once more packed. I had to let the people in because they were creating a disturbance in the street. For the first time I began to get panic-stricken myself wondering how long I could cope with the extraordinary situation. I tried to sit down for half an hour but the telephone, with its one-track enquiries, was in no mood for reprieves.

At half-past four I thought I had better make a start with Bert Wilcox or I should never get finished.

A quarter of an hour before midnight I locked the waiting-room door.

And it was evening and it was morning. The second day.

Three

Looking back it was possible to see the amusing side of the situation. At the time it was not the slightest bit funny. I never knew I had so many patients. It seemed that the entire practice came to the surgery morning and evening. I administered so many vaccinations I dreamed that I was still doing them even in my sleep. The nightmare persisted for three weeks. What happened to all the other aches and pains during this time is a mystery. Everyone was so preoccupied with the smallpox scare that they forgot about them. Unless, of course, they couldn't get near enough to tell me about them. It affected us all. Robin and I, of course, bore the brunt, working until all hours of the night to catch up; Miss Nisbet battled manfully with the telephone, both lines of which were jammed practically all day, and Sylvia took over when she had gone home.

In the second week the twins went back to school. This resulted in the presentation within two days of almost all the children in the school whom we had not as yet vaccinated.

'We thought we'd better bring them,' the

mothers said, 'since Penny and Peter have been done.'

I confronted Penny in the bath. 'What's all this about having been vaccinated?'

'What do you mean?'

'You've told all your chums that you and Peter have been vaccinated and it's made a lot of extra work.'

'Their mothers told them to ask. We have been done anyway.' She looked at the tiny white scar on her arm.

'When.'

'When we were babies.'

'You know perfectly well that's not what they meant.'

'Well, we got fed up with being asked. Anyway why can't we be? Everyone else is.'

'Thanks to you!'

There was now an adequate supply of vaccine and we just plugged solidly on. The pile of yellow forms mounted crazily. I sent patients down for more. Fired with a sense of emergency, misplaced in my opinion, they co-operated manfully.

On Robin's night off the queue in the waiting-room moved more slowly than ever.

'A bit unhygienic, what!' Major Pomfret said, as I blew a drop of vaccine on to his arm and made a scratch through it.

'A commonly used method,' I said, 'and not as bad as it looks.'

It was the most satisfactory method of

administering the vaccination and Major Pomfret was the first to comment.

Mr Greville, of Greville, Chalk and Jones, came in next. He was carrying a parcel.

'Jacket off,' I said, undoing a new vial.

'No, off with yours,' Mr Greville said.

'Look I've no time for jokes. I haven't eaten yet.'

'Neither have I. I've been waiting out there for an hour and a half. I've brought your suit.'

I remembered. Mr Greville's mother had been to stay with him and I'd diagnosed and treated her acute pancreatitis. Some weeks ago, bringing his tape-measure to the surgery, Mr Greville had measured me for a suit.

He took it out of the box, threaded here and there with long runs of white cotton.

'I don't know,' I said doubtfully, 'the waiting-room is still full.'

He held the coat. 'Coat off.'

I did as I was told. He held the new jacket, a beautiful thornproof tweed. I put my arms into it. He took one professional look and ripped out a sleeve disdainfully. Squatting, he slashed me here and there with white chalk; impaled me with pins.

'Lovely fit, lovely. Want to show the wife?'

'I simply haven't the time.'

'Let her have a look. Lies beautifully on the shoulders.'

I didn't want to upset him.

'Sylvia!' I called, looking at my one-sleeved, one shirted self in the hall mirror. 'Come and look.'

She was upstairs. 'How long will you be? I've prepared *Crème St Germain* and *côtelettes d'agneau Marie Louise* and everything will be done to a frazzle.'

'I'm not nearly ready.'

She stood on the stairs. 'What are you playing at now?'

'Like it?'

'Miss Nisbet said you've still over twenty people in there.'

'So I have.' Greville insisted. 'The finest thornproof with the compliments of Greville, Chalk and Jones. How's the back?'

'Fine.'

'See you in an hour.'

General Practice had its compensations. Mr Greville's was the first bespoke suit I had been given but over the years I had been handsomely treated by my patients. Mrs Peck was in handbags, Mr Collins in car accessories, Mrs McClean in children's clothes. Apart from actual gifts we had an entire range of household services at our disposal, gratis or at nominal charges. True, I fixed Ginger Johnson's boils while he fixed our plumbing and resolved Ernie Bolt's marital problems while he top-coated the sitting-room but we did know where to go

39

when it was a question of fuses, breakdowns or restoration and repairs anyway in the house or garden. 'You look after me, Doc I'll look after you.' This applied also to the butcher's where we were given the finest cuts by Sid, whose duodenal ulcer I had treated, to the greengrocer's where the finest fruit came our way from an inexplicably grateful Mrs Parsons whose husband I had been unable to save from carcinoma of the colon and to the sweetshop where Mr Pennyquick always slipped in a few extra for the kiddies.

The thornproof basted to his satisfaction, Mr Greville put it back in the box and rolled up his sleeve. 'Might as well since everyone else is.'

At ten past ten we closed the doors.

'I don't think I can stand it much longer,' Miss Nisbet said. 'Ronald's getting very angry.'

'Surely we must have vaccinated the entire practice by now.'

Miss Nisbet shook her head. 'Three hundred and twenty-nine.'

'Is that all?'

'That's all.'

I tried to think how many half crowns that was.

'You run along home now.'

'Thank you!' Miss Nisbet said. I noticed the bags under her eyes.

'I'm sorry about this.'

'It's not your fault. It's just that I don't know what Ronald will say.'

'Perhaps it's nearly over. There haven't been any new cases reported since the weekend.'

'Perhaps. Good night, Doctor.'

'Good night, Miss Nisbet. Thank you for your help.'

No sooner had I locked the door behind her than the telephone rang. I refused, I absolutely refused to do a single further vaccination that night. It was not a request for vaccination however but a message from Mrs Kahn's landlady asking if I could come as soon as possible. 'She looks,' Mrs Petersen said, 'not very good.'

I checked the supply of pethidine in my case and set out. Mrs Kahn was a dying woman and I had given her my solemn promise that I would not allow her to die alone.

Of all the sad stories, and in my profession there was no lack of them, Eugénie Kahn's was perhaps one of the most sad. She had moved into a one-roomed flatlet in Mrs Petersen's house some two years ago and took in sewing and alternations in order to earn a living. She was tall, blonde and beautiful with perfect bone structure and in the poorly furnished flat, with her innate elegance, she looked like a fish out of water. To see her you would not guess her history. I took to her at my first visit. Despite the

41

fact that she had such a severe pain in her side and was lying on the floor scarcely able to speak, she smiled at me with her eyes. She was in her late thirties I guessed and her room was a clutter of fragments of material, sewing machine and basted garments on headless dummies.

'I think it's bad, Doctor,' Mrs Petersen said when she let me in. 'She can't speak for the pain; I couldn't even get her on the bed. I told her you were the best doctor in the district!'

Smiling I went up the stairs.

'Pain!' was all she could say in a foreign accent, 'Bad pain.'

I examined her as best I could and made a tentative diagnosis of gall-bladder colic which could be most severe.

I filled a syringe with pethidine. She was wearing a white blouse buttoned at the wrist. I undid the buttons, pushed up her sleeve and quite suddenly some twenty odd years of history caught me unawares. On her arm was tattooed a visible instance of man's inhumanity to man, seven numbers long. Was it Bergen-Belsen or Theresienstadt, Auschwitz or Ravensbrück? Did it matter?

Slowly, with the pethidine, the pain eased. I pulled down her sleeve over the insult and when she became calmer helped her onto the bed.

She did not tell me her story that time, not

all at once. But over two years we had become friends. She did all Sylvia's alterations for her and she spent many evenings with us.

It turned out to be Bergen-Belsen. 'They called me the "rag-picker",' she told us, smiling just a little. 'I'd always been interested in clothes and I think scavenging for bits and pieces, less than bits and pieces, scraps you would call them, kept me going. My most treasured possession was a needle; I had to keep it hidden.'

She told me on various occasions about her life under the Nazis. For the most part she made light of them and spoke of people whose ordeals were far worse than her own. She kept a black and white baby panda on the chest next to her bed. One day I picked it up, not thinking. What she told me that day made me quail. It was the only time I heard her speak with hatred. When she was taken to the concentration camp she had a husband and baby of one year old. Her husband, who was not a very fit man, succumbed to starvation and ill-treatment during the first six months; she was left with her baby for whom she begged, borrowed and stole to keep her alive.

'I was determined,' she said, 'that Solange and I would survive. By observation I was able to deduce that the determination to survive was half the battle. I never left Solange; not for a minute; she was a bag of bones with

43

big blue eyes which trusted me. Some of the guards were kind, once they gave her chocolate. One day they posted a real beast in uniform to our block. He said I was to join a working party. I explained I could not leave Solange. Leave her in the hut, he said, she would be well looked after. Alone? I laughed. I should not have laughed. He put down his rifle, pulled Solange from my arms and hurled her head first with all his might to the ground.' She looked at the panda. 'I had to prise him from her arms. It was my husband's present to her for her first birthday. His name's Napoleon.'

I returned it gently to its place by her bed.

Eventually I said, 'Perhaps you will marry again. Have another child?'

'They had not finished with me. I was ill, they said, and transferred me to the hospital block where they sterilised me. That was my war!'

It might have been her war but her battle was not over. Investigations showed that she had lived through so much hardship to become a victim of cancer, a slow and extensive one. She had demanded to know the truth of her condition and I had told it to her. She was unperturbed. 'When you have lived where death is as commonplace as shopping or cooking, you are not afraid. But in the camp we were all companions in death. The only thing that scares me is to die alone.'

'Don't worry,' I said. 'I'll get you into hospital when the time comes.'

She held her hands over her eyes. 'Please, I beg you, Doctor, no hospitals. I tremble to think of one.'

She had no relatives, few close friends, I promised that come what may I would be with her in the terminal stages of her illness.

Stopping the car outside the Petersens' house I guessed that time had come.

By the look in her drugged eyes as I entered the room, scattered with its customary bits of material, I saw she knew it too. I took out the pethidine slowly.

She turned her eyes towards Napoleon sitting placidly in his customary position.

'Please!' she said, so that I could just catch the words. 'For your children.'

I said nothing. Penny and Peter were too old for toy pandas. Perhaps she had forgotten.

'There will be others,' she said, reading my thoughts, 'little ones!'

I took the furry animal which had seen so much sadness and put it next to my case. I read the number I knew now by heart on her arm for the last time and injected the drug to ease the pain. She closed her eyes and almost at once Cheyne-Stokes breathing began. This was the end. I had barely an hour to wait until the room became utterly silent. I, who was no believer in an after-life, hoped she was with Solange. I called for Mrs Petersen and picked up my case and Napoleon with his black patches by his ear.

All the way home I heard her voice in my ears. 'There will be others; little ones!' I hadn't told her there could be no others. After the birth of the twins, during which she had been ill, Sylvia had been told it was too dangerous for her to undergo a further pregnancy. We had a boy and a girl and were grateful. Occasionally, at the Zoo, or the circus at Christmas time, I'd catch her though, looking wistfully at a clustering quartet or an arguing trio and knew what was in her mind. I hid Napoleon in a drawer of my surgery desk and covered him with Final Certificates.

Sylvia put a steaming plate of soup in front of me. For a moment I sat motionless thinking of past events.

'Eugénie is dead,' I said.

'Oh no!'

We sat staring at each other. Life must go on. I picked up my spoon.

'What's this?' I said.

'*Crème St Germain.* I told you,' Sylvia sniffed, weeping quietly into her soup.

'No this!'

I held up a messy glass vial.

'Vaccine,' Sylvia sniffed through the tears which were rolling down her face. 'It must have fallen in from the fridge.'

Four

It was February before we realised it. The first batch of vaccinations had taken, or not, blistered or not, reacted or not and had been forgotten. At dances it was fashionable to wear sticking plaster on the arm. The scare was dying down. Vaccinations to other complaints now stood at one to ten instead of ten to one. It was the beginning of the end of an epoch none of us would easily forget. It ranked with the measles epidemic of five years previously and outdid the winter when everyone, but everyone, had flu. *Peu à peu,* as they say, the surgeries shrank to normal proportions and the visiting lists shrivelled to their customary winter lengths. I was sick to death of bared, anticipatory shoulders and did not want to see, for a long long time, another yellow card.

'What shall we do with the money?' Sylvia said, who hated to keep it.

'I don't know. You see before you a broken man. Anyway we haven't got it yet and shan't until next quarter.'

'But we will get it.'

'I sincerely hope so. I just hope I shan't be the richest man in the graveyard.'

'Stop being so morbid. You slept all night last night.'

'Most people sleep all night every night. You've forgotten that. I don't know why I ever took on this rotten job.'

'You know you love it.'

'I know.'

'We'll go away.'

'How do you mean?'

'With the money.'

'What money?'

'The money we haven't got. I'll tell you what. We'll go to Paris.'

'What about the children?'

'We'll take them with us. What a good idea. We'll take them to Paris in the holidays for their birthdays. They get a month at Easter. Do you realise they've never been abroad?'

'How many vaccinations do you think we've done?'

'Millions.'

'I must say it seems like it. Five hundred and thirty-three. Between Robin and myself, not to mention the Inland Revenue. Work that out a half-a-crown a scratch and we shan't get farther than Dover.'

'Never mind the vaccinations,' Sylvia said, 'I'm fed up with hearing about them. The twins will be thrilled to bits.'

'What about Robin? You can't expect him to share your enthusiasm.'

'He can have a holiday first. He doesn't

have to take school holidays.'

'I just feel like doing two people's work!'

'You'll be all right in a day or two. Things are just getting back to normal.'

I had lost half a stone and so had Robin. Miss Nisbet looked as if she could do with six weeks in the Bahamas. 'No fresh cases of smallpox reported' the newspapers said. For weeks they had carried pictures of queues at surgeries and health centres. The nightmare really seemed to be over. None of us dreamed that another would immediately replace it.

It started, like most nightmares, slowly and silently in the night. Unsuspectingly we slept. The practice slept too. No one had late night dramas or pains in the small hours.

It was Peter who brought it to our notice.

'Hey, Dad!' he said, in his pyjamas at six forty-five, 'Are you awake?'

'I am now.'

He drew back the curtains dramatically. 'Well look!'

I looked. The sky was grey. 'I'm looking.'

'No. On the ground. You'll have to get out of bed.'

'Not likely. You tell me.'

'Snow! It's six feet deep.'

'How do you know?'

'It comes halfway up the gate-post.'

That made it eighteen inches which was bad enough.

'May we go out and play?'

'You can go and clear the path so that I can get the car out.'

Sylvia grunted.

'What's that, dear?'

'No spade,' she said, turning over.

I thought she was dreaming of bridge then realised she meant to shovel up the snow.

'You'll have to use the broom,' I said.

'We really wanted to make an enormous snowman.'

'Well clear the path for Daddy first, there's a good lad.'

There were whoops of joy from outside the bedroom window. Not whooping I got up to inspect the extent of the newest hazard.

I had never seen so much snow. Our suburb slept beneath an uninterrupted blanket of white more reminiscent of Switzerland than subtopia. There were four visits already from the previous day, not one of them within walking distance. The first job would be to get the car out.

Bathed and dressed I realised that my wellington boots were in the garage.

I opened the front door and was hit by a blast of chill air.

'Will you get my boots from the garage, Pete? It'll come right over these shoes.'

Penny and Peter, noses running, breath steaming, looked at each other then at the garage. They looked at me. I looked at the garage. It had disappeared.

From the drive they had swept the snow up against the garage doors. They languished behind a Mont Blanc of it nine feet high.

'It's taken us an hour!' Penny said. 'Hasn't it, Pete?'

'It's awfully kind of you but how am I supposed to get to the car; or to my wellington boots? Kindly remove the snow and put it on the garden.'

Peter laid down his broom. 'I'm tired. It's jolly hard work.'

'So am I,' Penny said. 'And hungry.'

By breakfast-time I was soaking wet and exhausted. I had achieved my boots which were cold and clammy inside from their months of residence in the garage and my car which I had got no further than the rose-beds in which it was now, having skidded sideways when I got it out, firmly embedded.

'Ring Smithy at the garage, there's a good girl,' I said to Sylvia, shifting Penny's and Peter's coats and gloves and socks and scarves from the boiler and trying to find room for my own equipment.

She came back when I was drinking my coffee. 'Smithy's been out since dawn hauling people out. Just look at those puddles on the floor.'

'Never mind the puddles. Try the AA.'

'I have. They're permanently engaged.'

'Well if I can't get the car out I can't do the visits. Has anyone telephoned yet?'

'Fifteen visits.'

'You're joking!'

'I'm not. Some of them would have come to the surgery but they can't come out because of the snow.'

'I suppose,' I said hurrying with the coffee, 'I had better get started.'

I need not have hurried. In the surgery there was no Robin, no Miss Nisbet and no patients.

I went out to sit once more abortively in the car listening to the wheels spin merrily in the rose-beds.

'Can I help you, Doctor?' Robin said through the window. He was wearing a balaclava helmet.

'Where the hell have you been? Where's your car?'

'I had to leave it at the bottom of the hill. It's impossible to get up here. What exactly are you doing in the flowerbeds?'

'Stop being funny and give me a push.'

'What do you think I am? Hercules? This car weighs about a ton.'

'Never mind; push.'

He pushed going purple in the face, which went ill with the yellow balaclava. The wheels spun.

'Ask Sylvia for some salt.'

Penny and Peter, wrapped to the teeth, came out with the tea tray.

'What are you doing?'

'Going to school. 'Bye, Dad!'

They sat on the tray outside the gate and slid off down the hill.

Half a drum of table salt was all Sylvia was able to provide. It was useless. We tried sacking under the back wheels. The car was now at right angles to the drive.

Mr Howard and Mr Webster in galoshes and bowler hats were ploughing their way down the road.

'In trouble, Doctor?'

They came to help. So did the milkman who had arrived skidding in his float and the postman scarved to the eyes.

We managed to get it out into the road. Mr Howard and Mr Webster, a little the worse for wear, doffed their bowlers, the milkman and the postman went on their way.

'There's someone in the waiting-room,' Sylvia said.

It was Mrs Plumb holding her ankle and moaning.

'How did you manage to get here in the snow with an ankle like that?' I said.

She gave me a scathing look. 'I didn't. I came for my husband's certificate and slipped on your surgery steps! No doubt you'll be hearing from my solicitors!'

That was the next job. Robin and I swept the snow away and, reduced now to the dining-room salt cellar, sprinkled salt on the steps.

It was a day and a half. From every visit I made I had to be dug out. In practically every house I went to there was hardship; no coal, no coke, blocked wastes, frozen pipes. In some roads the mains themselves had frozen and the houses were completely without water. It was a Siberian scene.

I lunched off an omelette which was horrible.

'No salt,' Sylvia said. 'You put it all on the steps.'

It was only the beginning. The next day there had been another fall of snow and it was colder. The house was freezing.

'Put some fires on!'

'No electricity,' Sylvia said. 'There must be a power cut.'

We were all electric. We had no heat, I couldn't shave and had to drink orange squash with my cold breakfast.

Mrs Hodge's Jenny with swollen glands and a high temperature was my first visit.

'Terrible day,' Mrs Hodge said opening the door.

'Frightful. It makes it so difficult to get about. Not only that but we've had a power cut.'

'That doesn't worry us,' Mrs Hodge said. 'We're gas; not that the pressure's very good. There's always that trouble with electric.'

'You're quite right.' I followed her up the stairs. 'We cook by electricity. I haven't even had a cup of coffee this morning!' I hoped my voice was loud enough.

'Jenny's had a rotten night,' Mrs Hodge said. 'She really has, haven't you, Jen? Look how flushed she looks, poor kiddy.'

My words had fallen on the wind.

Jonathan Dean had lower abdominal pain, a slightly raised temperature and seemed to be cooking up an appendix. I telephoned the ambulance.

'They'll come for him as soon as they can, Mrs Dean. The road conditions aren't very good.'

'My husband walked to the station. I wonder how long this is going to last. I had better get Jonathan's things packed.'

It was useless mentioning the coffee.

Mrs Stockyard had the kettle on. I could hear it whistling.

'That's a merry sound,' I said listening to Mr Stockyard's chest. 'The kettle I mean. We've had a power cut. I haven't even had a cup of coffee yet this morning.'

'You poor soul,' Mrs Stockyard said. 'The minute you've finished with Mr Stockyard you come right down into the kitchen. You must be frozen.'

I smiled pathetically.

I had coffee, two enormous cups and half a packet of Dad's Cookies. After that I felt better.

Mrs Lime and Mrs Morton had heard

about our power cut and insisted on coffee. Mrs Cole from Ohio wouldn't let me go until I'd drunk a hot chocolate. By lunchtime I was floating.

Lunchtime! Sylvia carried a plate of gluey spaghetti from over the road where they cooked by gas. We huddled round the boiler in the kitchen together with the washing which she was attempting to dry.

On the last strand of spaghetti Mr Webster collapsed in his Men's Wear shop. I left the car on the hill having managed, with only two skids, to get there reasonably quickly. I rushed round to the boot for my case. It was stuck; frozen solid. A policeman with a red nose stood with his hands behind his back watching my abortive efforts.

'Can you read, sir?' he said finally.

I looked up wondering what the hell he was talking about.

He jerked a thumb to a notice above his head. 'No parking this side today.'

It was all I needed. Making a valiant attempt to keep my language moderately civil I explained my predicament. Together we forced open the boot and I was able to deal with Mr Webster who seemed to be having an internal haemorrhage.

The weather persisted for three weeks causing minor discomforts to myself and real hardship amongst many of my patients particularly the elderly ones who were frequently unable to get about in the snowy conditions. The only ones who really lived it up were Penny and Peter. Each day was a party with tobogganing and snowballs.

The mess was fantastic. The waiting-room was a constant swamp of dirty, melted snow. The kitchen steamed perpetually with drying shoes and garments. The carpets were trodden in with the red grit which had been laid in the road outside by the Council. I had more rides in more cars than at any time in my life. Mine was not good on snow and I frequently had to abandon it and accept lifts in smaller models with front wheel drives. Each visit was an expedition from which I was doubtful about my return. I was dug out, pushed out, hauled out and shoved out from every road in the district. The wipers froze, the windows froze, the heater made no impression. I bought a sheepskin jacket and a pair of fur-lined boots and did the visits looking like a mad Russian. Ambulances were late, half the people couldn't get out for prescriptions, district nurses froze on their bicycles.

I worried about the nights. It was often difficult to get the car out without help despite the spade and sacking with which I had equipped myself and which came on my visits with me. I could not guarantee speed in an emergency. Fortunately there were none on my duty nights and Robin, with a car which was better in the snow, coped with his.

Together with the milkman, the dustman, the postman and the baker, with whom our camaraderie was greater than ever as we traversed the snowy wastes, we battled on. Each visit took the energy of three, each journey the time of two. Each day we looked for a break in the grey sky, each night for a sign that the thaw had arrived.

When it did it brought with it burst pipes and fog. By day I visited houses knee-deep in mopping up; by night I walked to visits unable to see my case which dragged down by my side.

Sinuses became inflamed. The bronchitics coughed. The old people, hanging on to life by a thread through the preserving snow, succumbed. Ancillary services were working overtime and the hospitals were chock-a-block.

Sylvia brought home a brochure: 'Paris in the Spring!'

Five

Things, as they are wont to do, improved. As the vaccination scare passed, so did the snow, and finally leaving behind, according to Sylvia, filthy curtains, so did the fog. All that remained to remind us of the chaos were the scarred arms and the potholes left in the roads by the appalling conditions.

I suppose it was because I had been so preoccupied with battling against the elements that I hadn't noticed, until now, how very oddly Sylvia was behaving. There were two immediately apparent symptoms of her condition. The first was simple. Whenever I wanted her I couldn't find her. Not straight away that was. She had always been moderately visible, busy in the kitchen or sitting-room, now she kept hiding herself away. Her personality seemed, too, to have undergone a change; it was hard to say in what precise way except that she had become remote. If I spoke to her, when I did happen to locate her, she answered, but through a cloud as it were. If I asked her a question she'd look at me uncomprehendingly for a while then make a visible effort to collect her scattered thoughts sufficiently to answer. I began to get worried. She took to locking herself in. In the bedroom, in the bathroom, sometimes in the children's rooms. When I thought about it I realised that it had been going on for quite some time. I had simply been too busy for it to sink in.

The morning I discovered what she was up to was a particularly frustrating one. Kevin Hawkins aged eight weeks almost drowned from the fluid in his lungs, Margaret Powell, sixteen and unwed, went into labour, and Lucy Gunner made an attempt upon her life. Robin, of course, was at the hospital. It was always the way. When we were both around we scrupulously divided the half dozen visits between us. When only one of us had to cope all hell was let loose.

Two of the three urgent calls were something of a Chinese puzzle and it was just as well that they arrived, esoterically as they did, on a morning when I happened to be feeling quite bright. I was in the surgery examining an ear when Miss Nisbet came in with a repeat prescription to be signed.

'How are we doing?' I said, scrawling 'otitis media' on Patricia Dankworth's notes. 'Many visits?'

'Thirty-eight Essex and five Fitzroy children with sore throats and temperatures, Margaret Powell's been having pains on and off all night, Mr Forest has his back again,

Mrs Hawkins says Kevin's a funny colour and…'

'What do you mean a funny colour?'

'She didn't say.'

'Did she say it was urgent?'

'No, just to tell you.'

'You should have let me speak to her.'

I signed the prescription. 'Ring Mrs Hawkins for me.'

'Her telephone's out of order, Doctor. She rang from the call box.'

'How long ago?'

'About half an hour. She didn't sound worried.'

I was. Sometimes an urgent message meant nothing; an innocuous one sent alarm bells detonating through my brain.

'I'll shoot round there as soon as we're finished.'

'You've still about a dozen people…'

Just then the telephone rang on my desk to where Miss Nisbet had switched it when she left her office. She was nearest to the instrument while I was over by the window prescribing for Patricia's ear.

'I'll take it,' I said. I shall never know what made me utter them, but on those words rested the second life I was to save that morning.

I picked up the receiver. Before I had a chance to say anything at all a voice said, 'Please come!' Then the line went dead.

That was all.

'Anything the matter?' Miss Nisbet said.

Had she answered it that would have been that. No name, no message, no address. There was however no mistaking the voice of Lucy Gunner. I finished the prescription and gave it to Mrs Dankworth.

'Back in ten minutes,' I said to Miss Nisbet.

I was three hours.

Lucy Gunner was a symbol of the times; times which had moved too far too fast and in which the pressures more and more frequently became intolerable. Together with an increasing number of patients, young and old, in our practice, Lucy Gunner was depressed. There were so many pressures with which we now had to live; so many golden carrots held out by the mass-media; so much to confuse. It was I suppose hardly surprising that all around us women, surrounded by seemingly unconquerable mountains of household chores, wept quietly into the washing up; men sat in the waiting-room and when their turn came held out eager hands for magic drugs to save them from cracking up. The percentage of psychological problems with which we had to deal had increased with alarming rapidity. The less severe cases wanted help, the worst ones to be dead. I was lucky to have as my partner Robin to whom psychotherapy was the breath of life. He held a clinical assistant-ship in the department of psychological medicine at a teaching hospital to which he trotted off two mornings a week and in the light of his special knowledge he dealt with as many of the problems as he could cope with among our patients.

Lucy Gunner came first to me. I hadn't seen her before and as she sat, perfectly still, before my desk, it was a sight in which a Degas or a Renoir would have, I am sure, rejoiced.

'Have you just moved into the district?' I asked, enjoying the scenery.

'No.' Her voice was like fine gravel. 'But I've heard about you. I thought perhaps you could help.'

'I'll try,' I said, and thought what a pleasure it was going to be. She was one of the most beautiful women I had seen off the cinema screen. 'What's troubling you?'

It was quite a while before she replied. I waited, admiring the shape of her nose. She didn't twist her hands or look out of the window or fidget. Just sat there perfectly still.

'I feel my life is finished,' she said eventually in a flat voice. She was twenty-two.

'Tell me about it.'

'I wake up in the morning, and there's this dreadful feeling, hard to describe, a kind of heaviness. There's nothing I want to do;

nothing that seems worth doing; no point in talking to anyone, getting up, living. It's quite frightening.'

'Carry on.'

'I tell myself I have everything to live for. Harry … my husband, we have a two-year-old, Mark … I look at him and think What's the point? What's the point of anything? In the shops I look round the shelves; nothing has any meaning, food, dresses … I can't get interested…'

'How long has this been going on?'

'I don't know. For quite a while now. I'm afraid … that's why I came. Harry doesn't know.'

'Afraid of what?'

She didn't answer.

I waited, aware of the shuffling crowd in the waiting-room but knowing this was important.

'I might do something stupid.'

I knew what she meant. 'Had you considered it?'

'Yes.'

'And the means?'

'There are razor blades in the bathroom cabinet. Sometimes I lie on the bed and think how easy it would be.'

'What has stopped you?'

'It was too much effort to get off the bed and go into the bathroom. I'm scared though I might make the effort.'

'Have you told your husband about this?'

'Harry doesn't understand. He's been patient. I haven't gone out, asked anyone in. I can't. He tells me to snap out of it. He bought me a bracelet, emeralds, my birth stone, to cheer me up. It's beautiful I suppose. I look at the green stones trying to make them mean something, telling myself they're precious.'

'You have a mild depression,' I said, 'we can certainly help you.'

'I don't think so. You can't imagine how I used to be. Gay, night-clubs, dancing till the small hours. Everything is finished. I shall never be the same.'

'There are new drugs now specifically for your condition. I'd like you to make an appointment to see my partner. Dr Letchworth is an expert in these problems. Tonight? After evening surgery.'

She shrugged. 'He won't be able to do anything.'

'You may be pleasantly surprised.'

This was three months ago. Lucy Gunner, according to Robin, had been uphill work. About ten days ago he had happily reported that she was beginning to see the light, to take an interest once more in the normal processes of living.

She lived on the other side of town. In a large house where her bathroom was pink marble and her surroundings as beautiful as

65

she was herself. Everything seemed to be in my way; a pram on every zebra crossing, red at every traffic light, road works where I had reckoned on making up for lost time.

The front door of the Gunners' house, elegant between two potted bay trees, remained impervious to my knocking and ringing. I pushed open the side gate and was pounced on by a large dog who wagged his tail and followed me into the Ideal-Homes kitchen, through the unlocked back door.

'Mrs Gunner! Mrs Gunner!' My voice was blotted by the thick pile of the carpet.

'Mrs Gunner!' Upstairs I wondered which door. I flung open a few, nursery, bathroom, closet. Through the next I saw a king-size bed. On it in a beige chiffon something-or-other lay Lucy Gunner apparently lifeless. Beside her the telephone receiver burped rudely. There was no blood. She was practically pulseless. Under the bed I found what I was looking for; a smoky bottle on which the label read 'Mrs Gunner, one tablet three times a day.' It was empty. I rang the emergency ambulance and the local hospital to say she would be coming in and need immediate treatment. Bob Hurst, whom I knew well, was on duty. 'Drug overdose,' I said. 'I don't know how many she had. I'll try to contact Robin. Get everything laid on, there's a good chap.'

The ambulance came quickly, its bell

ringing. Across the road the curtains parted. A neighbour seeing Lucy on the stretcher said, 'Oh my God, what's happened?' and asked if there was anything she could do. I told her to contact Harry Gunner and tell him where we were taking his wife.

'Will she be all right?'

'I sincerely hope so.'

I went back into the house to try to contact Robin. As usual the hospital didn't answer. I hung on, drumming my fingers impatiently on the marble table in the hall.

'St Saviours. Can I help you?'

'Psychiatric out-patients. Quickly, please.'

'Everyone's in a hurry this morning.'

'Look, this is urgent.'

'They're engaged, speaking.'

'Interrupt the call, please. This is a suicide case.'

'You're through now, sir.'

'Hallo, Sister? Put me through to Dr Letchworth, please.'

'I'm sorry, Dr Letchworth is with a patient. Can I get him to ring you?'

I explained patiently.

'Hallo, Robin?'

'Where's the fire? I just had a little girl nicely hypnotised.'

I told him what had happened.

'I'll go straight over.'

'You needn't. Bob Hurst's on the job. I just wanted to know how many tablets she had and what?'

'Thirty-five Bellegron fifty mg. I gave them to her yesterday. She was doing so nicely.'

'I'll tell Bob.'

'Tell him I'll be right over.' He replaced his receiver.

There was nothing more I could do at the moment for Lucy Gunner.

I thought of the dozen people still waiting for me at the surgery and turned the car in the direction of home. Then I remembered Kevin Hawkins whose house lay in the opposite direction and for one of those inexplicable reasons turned the car once more.

'Kevin?' I said when Mrs Hawkins, in her dressing-gown and hair rollers, opened the door with her two-year-old in her arms.

'I wasn't expecting you until after the surgery. I'm sorry, everything's in rather a mess.'

'Don't worry. What seems to be the matter?'

I followed her up the stairs.

'I don't know really. When he woke up this morning he seemed to be very quiet; he didn't take his six o'clock feed and seemed a very odd colour. He's dropped off again now. It seems a pity to wake him.'

The baby's room was in darkness. I opened the curtains and looked in the cot. He was quiet all right, scarcely breathing, and white round the lips.

I picked him out of the cradle and

wrapped a blanket round him.

'What are you doing?'

I handed him to Mrs Hawkins. 'Bring him down quickly, we're going to the hospital.'

'I can't. What about Paul?'

'Bring him too.'

'I'm not dressed.' She put a hand to her head.

'Mrs Hawkins, Kevin is dying!'

I hadn't meant to be so brutal, only to get her moving. I picked up Paul who was too surprised to protest, and without another word Mrs Hawkins followed me down the stairs and out into the car.

The baby, eight weeks old, was suffering from acute laryngotracheo-bronchitis. It was a rapidly progressing condition culminating within a few hours into death from the waterlogged lungs. Frequently this occurred in the night. When the mothers discovered the babies in the morning it was too late. With Kevin we might just be lucky, but already he was practically moribund.

For the second time within the hour I drove with urgency, cutting in on the patiently waiting lines of traffic, rounding an island on the wrong side, crossing the lights at red.

At the admission doors I grabbed Kevin from Mrs Hawkins and rushed into Casualty.

'Where's Dr Hurst?'

'He's busy with an overdose.'

I had forgotten Lucy Gunner. Bob Hurst

came out of a cubicle.

'You again...' he looked at Kevin. 'That baby doesn't look too healthy.'

'Suck him out quickly, there's a good chap.' He took the baby and was away, the little nurse running after him.

In the cubicle Lucy Gunner lay motionless, a Ryle's tube down her nose. By her side was Robin.

'How on earth did you get here?'

'Helicopter.' He wasn't smiling.

'How's she doing?'

He shook his head. Having been responsible for her treatment it was no joke for Robin. I don't think I had ever seen him looking so completely serious.

I rang Miss Nisbet from Sister's desk. 'Keep everything on ice,' I said. 'I just want to wait and see what happens with the Hawkins' baby then I'll be back. Twenty minutes at the most.'

'I've been trying to contact you,' Miss Nisbet said. 'The midwife rang ten minutes ago. Margaret Powell's second staging.'

'You'd better send the patients home. Anything urgent I'll see at lunchtime. Ring the midwife and tell her I'll be over straight away.'

'I'll be round at the Powells',' I told Robin and gave him the thumbs up for Lucy Gunner.

Mrs Hawkins in her dressing-gown, tears

70

in her eyes, stopped me in the corridor.

'What are they doing to Kevin?'

'Dr Hurst is with him now. He'll do everything possible.'

'Will he be...?'

'I hope so, Mrs Hawkins.' I was sorry to
sound so brusque. 'I have to dash. There's
another emergency.'

A middle-aged man, dressed for the city,
came through the swing doors. In my haste
I almost knocked him over.

'Sorry,' I muttered, one foot on the porch.

'Just a moment, young man,' he said. 'I'm
Harry Gunner.'

Six

I was surprised. Lucy Gunner was twenty-two; this man for all his spruce appearance must be pushing sixty.

'Come this way,' I said, retracing my steps to the Casualty Department. 'Dr Letchworth is with your wife now.'

'Is she...?' His face was grey.

For the third time that morning I tried to project a reassurance, an optimism I did not feel.

Later, I heard the strange story of the Gunners. According to Robin, Harry Gunner until four or five years ago had been a happily married man with three grown-up children, one of whom was married with children of her own. One morning, so the story went, Harry Gunner, contented family man for thirty years, had looked at his wife across the breakfast-table. She wore a housecoat, as was customary for the time of day, and, uncorseted, bulged out both above and below the belt. Her hair was grey, but with a delicate blue weekly applied tint, and her face slackly contoured. Harry was reading *The Times*, a defence mechanism he had perfected over the years; his wife, complaining the while of

72

pains in her back, her front and her legs, was bemoaning the fact that the new curtains had turned out different to the pattern, her daughter was criminally careless about wrapping her grandchild up in the treacherous weather and their eldest son's latest girl friend refused to wear shoes. For some reason Harry Gunner was unable to explain, he had found himself looking from the woman who sat opposite to him at the breakfast-table to the photograph on the mantelpiece, somewhat dated it is true, of a young bride as fresh and promising as the gardenias she carried. Where, he wondered, did all the beautiful young brides go to and from where did all the battle-axes emerge? Not that his wife was exactly a battle-axe. She loved him, after her fashion, looked after his physical needs solicitously, laughed only occasionally and grumbled interminably. All at once, however, after thirty years, the woman behind the coffee-pot had become a stranger. He blinked to dispel the heretic thoughts that filled his brain. They stuck obstinately, refusing to be dispelled. That day he went about his usual business in the City. To his secret cerebrations he added another. Had he too become an elderly back number? He certainly did not feel it; his mirror denied it. He decided to confirm his own impressions. He began to smile at pretty girls. They smiled back; only to help him on with his overcoat, to give him their seats in the train. He felt a Lothario, they treated him like Lear. Until he met Lucy Brown. Lucy worked in the Florian Gallery to where Harry Gunner repaired one lunchtime in search of a painting whose acquisition was his hobby. He possessed already a Poussin, a Bonnard, several Manets and a Dufy. He had heard that at the Florian they had just acquired a Braque. No one had told him that they had also acquired Lucy Brown. She was standing near the window in the Gallery when he went in. He was familiar with ladies of beauty from the simpering Botticelli Venus to the more robust Mesdames of Rubens. Nowhere had he seen anyone more beautiful than Lucy Brown. She was tall and slim; yet not so slim that beneath the silver-grey sweater she wore over a matching skirt there were more than hints of exciting promise. Her eyes formed a three-piece with the rest of her outfit, her hair had darkened from a childhood blondeness and she had not troubled to recapture its golden-sovereign colour. She had merely wound it on to her perfect nape from where it set off a matchless mouth and wide cheekbones. She asked whether she could help him. He forgot about the Braque. He said it didn't matter and was about to leave the Gallery before she smiled at him with the sympathetic smile of youth for middle-aged men with which over the past weeks since his discovery he had become familiar. At that moment however Florian himself had appeared. 'Ah, Mr Gunner,' he said, 'we have your Braque in the far room. Miss Brown will look after you. If you will excuse me my parking meter has two minutes only to run and I have a luncheon appointment.' With that he left them. On such trivialities do convulsive happenings turn. While pondering upon his sudden change in attitude towards his wife who had become, over the years, a habit, Harry Gunner had not intended to indulge in anything more than harmless flirtation, imaginary even, with members of the opposite sex, in order to prove to himself his own continued appeal. That was, however, until he met Lucy Brown.

'It's very warm in the Gallery,' she said, 'would you like me to take your coat?'

For the moment he did not answer. He could not. Firstly he had not expected a matchless voice that did things to his legs to go with a matchless appearance. Secondly he wanted to delay the moment when she would smile with sympathy, the young tending the old, as she helped him off with his heavy overcoat.

When he did move he did not look at her. Just undid the buttons and felt her remove it from his shoulders. When he handed her his maroon silk scarf, however, he forgot his resolution. He looked into the deep grey eyes and found them, to his complete distractions, looking with neither sympathy nor indifference but with unmistakable interest into his. He did not buy the Braque. He did not even look at it. When Florian returned he had, on the sofa in the far room, finished telling Lucy about his thirty-year marriage and was listening sympathetically to the story of her desperately unhappy year with a handsome, compulsive gambler whom she had now divorced.

He had fought against it. Thirty years was thirty years. He was neither an unkind man nor one without principles. After a year of misery he knew that he had to have Lucy Gunner and loved her too much to make her his mistress. They had been married now for three years and his grandchildren were older than their son. He contributed in no way to Lucy's present condition. She was still as much in love with him as he with her and the circle within which they moved had accepted the discrepancy in their ages. Harry Gunner was not the first man to wish to recapture a lost youth. Few had done it more successfully.

I knew nothing of this however on that hectic morning when beautiful Lucy Gunner lay fighting for her life, or rather with Robin and Bob Hurst fighting for it, only that Harry Gunner seemed awfully old to be her husband.

I handed him over to Robin and set off to see what I could do for Margaret Powell.

Just as Lucy Gunner was in many ways a product of the times so too was Margaret Powell, at sixteen about to become a mother. Margaret's parents had been patients of mine for many years and were what was known as 'respectable'. This convenient label implied a neatly kept suburban house, a husband who sold insurance with moderate success and one daughter at the local Grammar School. Margaret, the nigger in the woodpile, having been too indolent to work for her eleven-plus examination, had found herself at the Comprehensive where she found no reason to revise her attitude to life. Her philosophy could be summed up in two words. 'Who Cares!' Both Mr and Mrs Powell wondered frequently what they had done to deserve this seemingly godless child utterly lacking in any spark of morality. She had, as far as her parents were able to judge, no redeeming features. Since a small child she had been unduly concerned with her appearance and in recent years the condition of her hair, nails and clothes appeared to have occupied her every waking thought. She was unable to leave for school in the mornings until before her mirror she had back-combed every strand of what might have been pretty hair and tortured it into some grotesque style. At night she never retired without a complete armoury of pins, nets and rollers set about her ears. Washing, if of any, was of secondary importance; not only her own face and body. According to Mrs Powell, whose despair over the years she had become, her underwear was a positive disgrace. To neat-as-a-pin Mrs Powell this slovenliness was a daily cross she had to bear. It was a light one compared with Margaret's philosophy. No one, according to Margaret, in this enlightened day and age, took the remotest notice of either parents or teachers; no one worked; why should they? No one occupied themselves with anything other than television, dancing and the opposite sex; what else was there that mattered? Squares went to church, fools had good manners and only unspeakable morons helped, in any way at all, at home. 'All my friends', according to Mrs Powell's Margaret, smoked, congregated outside the nearest tube station to discover where the night's diversion was to be found, and devoted every moment of every day saved from the pursuit of beauty to 'having a good time'. What else was life for? What sort of a time did teachers have walking home each day, disheartened, on well-worn soles to their semi-detacheds or bed-sitters? What sort of a time did parents, steady workers, have, devoted funlessly to duty? What joy was there in studying, slaving, putting one's shoulder to the wheel, when you could be shaking, twisting, hitch-hiking, sniffing in the company of one's hirsute idols? That's what life's for, Margaret said, to enjoy yourself. Where had all this crazy worrying, slogging, good-doing, preaching got anyone? It was every man for himself and spend all your money on clothes and cigs and chocs and a good time and try to find a boy with a bike and buy a skid-lid and get all the thrills and Southend on a Sunday and really feel the noise and the power of it filling your whole body, not like all those miseries saying 'disgusting' and turning their noses up and saying you're making too much noise and never thinking of anyone else. Why should you? They didn't think of you. If I am not for myself who will be for me? That's what's wrong with the world, nobody laughs enough and there's too much 'don't do this' and 'don't do that' and nobody can tell you *why* except that they never had a good time themselves, not in the other generations. They never knew how to and now they don't want you to enjoy yourself although they don't have a reason, just sour grapes. Who wants to spend all weekend washing dishes and visiting Gran just because she happened to be old, sitting in purgatory; and what was the point of all this arithmetic and English? You'd never use it, you could speak English already and never use those sums again, and the history was old hat just for books and libraries. Who cared what happened all those years ago out of the ark; the teachers were out of the ark too, liked to think they weren't, talking to you and saying they understood and times had changed and wanting to know what you were thinking. They'd have a fit if they knew, an absolute fit, and it wasn't times that had changed it was people, and they had more sense knowing that it was a short life and a sweet one and before you could say knife you were thirty and settled down and all those worries and another war even although war sounded fun and something to do so you might as well make the best. And best was boys. If you were a girl, that was. And the more money they had the better, they gave you a better time and Margaret was sixteen and most of the girls in her class had done it and it was what they talked about most of the time in the cloakroom in front of the spotted mirrors back-combing their hair with grubby combs and discussing where and who with and what was it like. They said you shouldn't, had teenage discussions on the telly sometimes. Very pompous clergy and leaders of youth-clubs and things but they could never tell you why. Probably that they hadn't and wished they had the chance and it all boiled down again to the same old thing. Anyway it was marvellous, not really to do with just anyone, but if you had one real boy and you liked each other, and where was the harm? Babies and that, but all the boys knew what to do and that disease but they'd never heard of anyone getting it, they said it just to frighten you. It was another of those things and it really was fun, a really good time until trouble, and not even Margaret Powell knew what had gone wrong. At first she had been pale and sulky, paler and sulkier than usual that was, and then off her food and they'd taken her to the doctor's, and that was me, saying did she need a tonic, and I'd given her one saying yes probably and that Margaret should come back in a day or two and tell me what effect it was having, preferably on her own.

'Well, Margaret?' I said, when she returned without her mother. She had on tight black trousers and black boots and she could scarcely see out of her eyes for hair and there was muck an inch thick on her face over the spots, and silver over the dirty nails.

'Well, what?'

'What's the matter?'

She looked at her boots.

'I'm scared.'

'What about?'

'I'm in trouble.'

'How do you know?'

She gave me a pitying look. 'The gypsies never told me!'

'Well before we go any further I'd better have a look at you.'

When she was on the couch I said, 'How many months pregnant do you think you are?'

'Nearly four.'

'Why didn't you do anything about it before now?'

'I did.'

'What?'

'I took some pills.'

'I didn't mean that. Where did you get them?'

'The chemist's. A girl friend told me.'

'What happened?'

'They made me dead sick. Nothing else.'

'Get dressed then and we'd better discuss it. You are of course going to have a baby.'

'Thanks for the info!'

Her scathing tone made me feel about a hundred. When she was sitting down I said: 'Have you told your parents yet?'

'You must be kidding? They don't know what it's for.'

'They did have you and your sister,' I pointed out.

'Gawd knows how. The way they talk you'd think it was something disgusting.'

'Why didn't you come and see me earlier?'

'I've been out of my mind. I took these pills like I said. I wanted to do what my friend did but I'm a coward. A shocking coward. I can't stand the sight of blood. Or pain. She nearly died.'

'What did your friend do?'

'She met this man in a pub in Ealing. Someone told her. He was quite old but not too bad and she gave him twenty quid. She didn't feel anything, not at the time, but afterwards it was terrible. I wasn't there, I couldn't, but her friend said. She was screaming in agony all night. He thought she was going to die. The man gave her some tablets. He does film stars and all those people. I couldn't... Would you have done something if I'd come here?'

'You know very well it's illegal. Who's the father?'

'A boy.'

'I gathered that. How old is he?'

'Seventeen.'

'Have you told him?'

'No.'

'Why?'

'He's got this other girl.'

'You weren't thinking of marrying him then?'

She looked as if I'd said a dirty word.

'Who wants to get married?'

'What's the objection?'

'Where's the fun of being married? Anything might happen. Not if you're married though.'

'Like what?'

She shrugged. 'I might end up in China, or with a lord, or have me name up in lights. Fantastic things. Look at my mother.'

'What about her?'

'She knows what's going to happen; every day. The milkman, the supermarket, washing the curtains, collecting green stamps, waiting for me Dad to come home, I'd go crazy.'

'Margaret, I think the time has come for you to face facts.'

I saw a mask of defence come over her face.

'I don't say you won't end up in China or marrying a lord but at the moment, at this very moment, you are four months pregnant. What are you going to do about it?'

Her mouth grew stubborn.

'The first thing you have to do, as you very well know, is to tell your parents.'

'They'd never believe it.'

'They love you. They do everything for your good.'

'I don't want to be done good. That's just the point. I want to live my own life. I can look after myself...'

'Can you?'

'Well all right. Something happened. A mistake. But love me! Don't make me laugh. I'm idle and useless and boy-mad and wicked. If I was like Anne now, helping with the dishes and stopping home nights

84

and weeding and shopping on a Saturday, but I'm not. I want to enjoy my life.'

'You have to tell them.'

'I'd rather die.'

'Don't be so melodramatic. They'll probably take it much better than you think. Parents are almost as much misunderstood as children.'

'What about the people in our turning? Me Mum wouldn't be able to face them. And what about me Dad – very respected at his job he is.'

'You tell them and I'll back you up if there's any difficulty.'

'Can't you tell them I got something wrong with me stomick?'

'I'm not telling them anything, Margaret. It's hard, I know. Perhaps the first really difficult thing you've had to do in your life. I'm sure you'll do it admirably.'

'I can imagine,' she said sarcastically. ''Evening, Dad, guess what? You're going to be a Grandpa! What'll I do with it anyway? Take it to school and put it on me peg?'

'One thing at a time. Tell your family first.'

'I'm scared. Of having it. Our neighbour was twenty-four hours in terrible agony my Mum said.'

'I'll look after you if you want me to.'

'Give me things? So I won't feel anything? Stay with me?'

'If you want me to. You probably underestimate yourself. Come back next week, let me know how you've got on, and we'll have another little chat.'

Seven

She returned the following week on the back of a motorbike driven by a young man with a beard. But not before I'd had a visit from Mrs Powell.

'About Margaret, Doctor!'

'Yes.'

'I never thought the day would come when a daughter of mine...'

'Mrs Powell,' I said.

'...brought it on herself with her short skirts and her boys and ironing her hair. Thinks the world owes her a living. Owes it to her; just like that. All she thinks of is getting rich, as if it's going to drop out of the sky. We've done our best, you know we have. You can't keep check. She's rude to me and ignores her father. If we ask her where she's been she says, "Can't you leave me alone, you're always nagging?" Nagging. Perhaps we should have done a bit more nagging, taken a stick to her like they used to...'

'Mrs Powell,' I said. 'Are you going to stand by Margaret? She needs you now, you know.'

'She should have thought of that before. No sense of decency. What do you think my neighbours would say? Can't she go away?'

'She can, yes.'

'She'd better go then.'

'She's only sixteen.'

'I'm quite aware of that, Doctor.'

'She needs her mother just now. I'm sure you won't let her down.'

'*Me* let *her* down? You aren't suggesting she stays at home?'

'That's exactly what I am suggesting. Unless you want her to have your grandchild amongst strangers who may be less than sympathetic. I'm sorry to say it again but she is only a child.'

'What about the baby?'

'I can arrange for adoption.'

'What about Fred?'

'You haven't told him?'

'He'd die of shame. He's held in very high esteem at Head Office, you know.'

'I'm sure you'll work something out together. And Mrs Powell–'

'Yes, Doctor?'

'Don't be too hard on Margaret.'

She sniffed. 'They want it all ways. The good time, the "laughs" as Margaret always says. And when they get what's coming to them you mustn't be too hard. Fred will murder her.'

But as I'd thought, Fred didn't murder her.

'What did your father say?' I asked

Margaret when she came back to see me.

'Read me the riot act. Common tart, should be ashamed, deserved to be thrown on the streets, scraped and saved for Anne and me, only wanted the best for me... I don't want the "best". Not their best anyway. A house in the suburbs, pay packet of a Friday and a herbaceous border. When I'm thirty perhaps, but you may as well be dead then anyway.'

'What did you decide?'

'I'm to have it at home. They're punishing themselves and me. I'm to see how I've humiliated them, brought disgrace on them, they're rubbing my nose in it...'

'Don't be hard on them, Margaret. It's a shock. They'll come round.'

I examined her and pronounced her fit and in need only of a few vitamins.

'Who's the boy?' I asked as she was going.

Her face lit up. 'That's Ted. He's from Wapping.'

As if that explained everything. I didn't ask if Ted knew about the baby.

Her pregnancy had been uneventful, medically that was. She had continued at school until her condition became obvious then stayed at home consuming pounds of chocolate for which she had a pica, sitting with her feet up in front of the fire and watching the telly. Her mother, with tightened lips, sat in the evenings behind the drawn curtains and knitted matinée coats. She also bought napkins and put a pram on order; all of which business Margaret ignored completely, engrossed in her soft centres and romantic serials in which she forgot her swollen belly and identified herself with the glamorous heroine. Disgrace had come to number thirteen Bridgemont Road, but its harbinger seemed not to care. She was unaware that her mother no longer shopped at mid-morning when the neighbours were about but crept out stealthily at closing time; if she noticed that Mrs Clarkson from number fifteen and Mrs Rogers from number eleven no longer popped in to borrow a cup of sugar or for a chat, she made no comment. She grew slowly fatter and more unkempt. The only outings she made were to my surgery for her monthly, fortnightly, and, recently, weekly check-ups at which I was able to assure her that everything, medically speaking, was as it should be. Against my wishes she was going to have her baby at home; on this Mrs Powell was adamant. She was not going to have her disgrace flaunted from the rooftops of the local hospital.

Now the time, according to the message Miss Nisbet had given me, had come. The door of number thirteen was ajar, presumably for my arrival, and the curtains of numbers eleven and fifteen swaying fractionally although there was no breeze.

I hung my coat over the banister; screams rent the air mingling with the smell of stale chips. 'Help! I'm dying. Where's the doctor?'

'Shut up, Margaret, we've all had them' – Mrs Powell's voice.

'Not like this you haven't. Help!'

The midwife, not one of my favourites, nor renowned for her sympathy and understanding, was going about her business in a precise and unhurried way. Mrs Powell was standing tight-lipped by the window and Margaret writhing in highly exaggerated agony on the bed.

I despatched Mrs Powell downstairs, obtained some relevant facts from the midwife then pulled a chair to the bed to have a word with Margaret whose ordeal was worse than anything she had imagined in her wildest dreams.

'Can't you get me something, Doctor? Put me out or something? I'm going to die, I know I'm going to die. Why didn't anyone tell me it was going to be like this? ... owwwwwwh!'

I waited for the pain to pass. When it had gone I put the mask of the gas and air apparatus into her hand.

'Now listen, Margaret, you're not dying. Everything is just as it should be and having a baby is not the most comfortable of procedures. You're a strong girl though and there's no reason why you shouldn't bring this baby into the world with perfect ease. The worst is almost over. All I want you to do is to relax; just relax. When you feel a contraction coming put the black mask over your nose and breathe in and out deeply through your mouth.'

She put the mask to her nose.

'No, not yet. You aren't having a pain yet.'

'But I might.'

'You have to wait.'

'You'll stay with me?'

I took her hand. 'Yes.' I thought of my full waiting-room. 'Yes, Margaret, if you promise to do exactly as I say I'll stay with you. No more of your nonsense though! Just take it very quietly and Nurse and I will help you.'

It was as well that I stayed. After a rather slow second stage during which Margaret grew too tired even to complain and even Mrs Powell began to get agitated, the foetal heart became weaker and I decided the time had come to put the forceps on under local anaesthetic. The child, a boy, was born dead. Watched by the reluctant grandmother and assisted by the midwife I tried all methods of resuscitation but there was obviously to be no success.

'I want to see my baby,' Margaret said.

'Why doesn't he cry?' Mrs Powell asked anxiously, looking at the little blue scrap of humanity and forgetting for the first time the voice of disapproval.

'I think we'll wrap him up, Nurse, and take him into the other room.'

I handed him to the midwife. Margaret's eyes followed me.

'He's dead, isn't he?'

'Yes. He's dead.'

Her tears dripped on to the pillow.

'Isn't it better like this, Margaret?'

She shook her head. For all her schoolgirl tantrums she was a woman with nothing to show for her efforts.

'There'll be others. In better circumstances.'

'I couldn't go through that! Not again I couldn't. Never. Are you sure he's dead?'

'Quite sure. I've tried everything.'

'I knitted some bootees. One, any rate.' She looked towards the dressing-table on which lay some grey-white knitting.

'One wouldn't have been much use.'

'I s'pose it wouldn't. No I s'pose it wouldn't. Not one wouldn't. Can you imagine walking down the street with one bootee...' She started to laugh hysterically, the tears pouring down her tired face which in the first flush of motherhood was almost beautiful.

I filled a syringe with ergometrine.

'Ouch!'

'There. All over. I think you should have a

little sleep now. You've worked very hard. I'll call in and see you later.'

Her eyelids were growing heavy.

'I think I shall call him Patrick,' she said her speech slurred. 'Patrick, after his Dad.'

In the front room Mrs Powell was sobbing unashamedly.

'You'll be able to hold your head up again, Mrs Powell,' I said perhaps unkindly. 'No illegitimate grandchild to explain away.'

'Such a tiny little scrap!'

'It's been rather a shock for Margaret. You'll have to help her to get over it. She'll need a lot of sympathy.'

'The Lord giveth and the Lord taketh away.'

'You may find her a little depressed. Don't scold her whatever you do.'

Mrs Powell looked injured. 'Me? Scold! I won't say a word.'

I sighed. 'She needs a word. Several words in fact; of kindness.'

'After what we've been through these last months...!'

'Try to think what Margaret's been through these last hours – with nothing to show for it. It's an immense psychological shock, Mrs Powell. There's bound to be some reaction. I've given her something to make her sleep but when she wakes up she's going to ask for her baby. You'll have to explain as gently as you can. Talk about the future. Give her

94

something to look forward to.'

Mrs Powell sniffed. 'Better mind her P's and Q's in future, that young lady had.'

I could see I was wasting my time, put on my coat and picked up my case.

'I'll look in again this evening. Ring me before if anything worries you.'

Outside the house a pimply youth in a skid-lid, straddling a motorbike and looking like something out of space stopped me.

'She 'ad it?'

'What's that?'

'Maggie. The baby?'

'Ah! You must be Patrick.'

He looked puzzled. 'Snorty. Well Ted really but they call me Snorty on account of me adenoids. Me and Margaret's going steady.'

'She's had the baby but I'm afraid it didn't live.'

'Can I see 'er?'

'I'm afraid you can't now, she's sleeping. Perhaps tomorrow.'

He plucked a bunch of not very bright looking roses from his saddlebag and flung them in the gutter. '...if 'e's dead, poor little bleeder...'

I stooped and picked them up. 'You give the flowers to Margaret. She'll appreciate them more than ever.'

I got into the car glad that salvaged from the wreck Margaret had at least Snorty and his wilted roses.

I hadn't realised how weary I was after my catastrophic morning. I was amazed on looking at my watch to see that it was almost four o'clock and wondered whether I would be too late for lunch or too early for tea.

I put my case down in the hall. I listened and could hear nothing but an eerie stillness. The waiting-room was empty, cleared long ago I presumed by Miss Nisbet and Robin and awaiting the evening onslaught. Penny and Peter I remembered were at Brownies and Cubs.

'Sylvia!' I yelled up the stairs.

No reply.

'Sylvia! Where are you?' She couldn't be out because we were on telephone duty. I sighed remembered her latest locking-herself-away habit and felt almost too weary, hungry and thirsty to start the game of hide-and-seek I frequently had to indulge in if I wanted to talk to my lawful wedded wife.

'Sylvia! Where the blazes are you?'

She was nowhere downstairs.

I went upstairs; bedroom, children's bedroom, ours tidy, theirs untidy, both empty.

The bathroom was locked.

'Sylvia!'

'Who is it?'

'Who do you think it is, Father Christmas? Open the ruddy door this minute or I'll kick it in.'

There was a rustling from within. 'Temper, temper!'

'I've had no lunch and no tea. Come to think of it,' I said self-pityingly, 'I haven't had any elevenses either!'

'Neither have you, Sweetie,' – she sounded all contrition – 'just hang on five seconds...'

'Don't sweetie me, open the door.' I leaned against it and she did. We both landed up on the bath-mat, Sylvia looking ridiculous with the horn-rimmed glasses she had lately needed to wear at the end of her nose.

'Look, this is ridiculous!'

'What is?'

'Firstly, I've had no lunch.'

She bridled. 'Whose fault is that? I made a perfectly good Bitkis in tomato sauce with black olives which has been slowly dehydrating in the oven all afternoon.'

'Secondly I've had no tea!'

She peered at her watch. 'It's only five to four.'

'Five!'

She pushed the glasses up her nose and looked again. 'Five then!'

'Thirdly the time has come for you to explain the meaning of your extraordinary behaviour.'

She looked decidedly shifty. 'I don't know what you mean.'

'You know perfectly well. You keep hiding yourself away; locking yourself in rooms and acting altogether in a thoroughly odd manner.'

'I do, do I?'

'Yes, if you must know. You do.'

'So?'

'So I want to know what you're up to.'

'I don't ask you what you're up to every minute of the day.'

'You know perfectly well what I'm up to; serving humanity, saving lives!'

She lay back against the bath and snorted.

'Well I am, as a matter of fact. But what you're up to heaven only knows.'

Sylvia looked at me long and hard and then seemed to come to a decision. 'If I tell you, you won't tell a soul?'

'Not a living soul!'

'Cross your heart.'

'Look, Sylvia, we're not fourteen…'

'All right, take it easy. As a matter of fact,' she looked towards the dirty linen-box, 'I'm writing a book.'

'Writing!'

'That's right.'

'You?'

She nodded.

'A book?'

She sighed wearily and opened the dirty linen-bin from which she extracted a mass of handwritten quarto sheets two inches thick and covered with her own quite appalling handwriting. She handed it to me and I glanced at a page a random.

'Sylvia!' I said. 'This is disgusting!'

'What is?' She peered over my shoulder. 'Oh that!'

'Yes, that. And this. And this, and this…'

She sighed again. 'You don't understand.'

'No, I don't. I'm not surprised you write in the bathroom.'

'You have to make them sexy these days or nobody reads them.'

'I didn't know you knew those words even.'

'Well I do; so there. Don't worry,' she said, 'I'll publish it under a pseudonym!'

'Publish!' I said, nearly falling into the bath with laughter. 'You aren't thinking of publishing this rubbish?'

'I'll have you know a publisher is already interested, keenly interested.' She pushed up her glasses which had again slipped down her nose.

'He is, is he? And what are you going to do, make our fortunes?'

She pushed the glasses firmly up her nose again.

'No,' she said, 'I'm going to buy some contact lenses!'

Eight

'What I don't understand,' I said, sitting on the edge of the bath, 'is what all the secrecy is for. You've been driving me crazy hiding yourself away like this.'

'I thought you'd laugh at me. Anyway you'd read it.'

'Correct me if I'm wrong but I thought that's what books are for.'

'Not until they're finished.'

'When will that be?'

'Not long now; provided no one gets measles or anything. He's practically got the girl.'

'Who has?'

'This doctor.'

'Doctor!'

'That's all I know about. Doctoring and modelling. The next one will be about modelling.'

'People will think it's me.'

'Not a chance.'

'Why?'

'This one's too sexy. He has a go at all the female patients. The pretty ones anyway. Gets away with it too, until nearly the end.'

'Then what happens?'

'I think I shall have him struck off,' she said languidly.

'How unpleasant!'

'He's not a very pleasant character.'

'What will he do then?'

'I hadn't really thought. Sell matches or something. It doesn't really matter because it won't be until the very end.'

'Thanks!'

'Don't take it all so personally. It has nothing to do with you. I'm sorry I told you. You'll be sorry too when I sell the film rights for millions of pounds.'

'I was only kidding. I think you're very clever, really I do. Now if you could just consign your over-sexed doctor to the linen-bin for a while perhaps you could summon up the energy to find this one something to eat.'

She put her arms round me. 'Poor darling!'

I pushed her away. 'Unlike Dr Linen-bin, I'm afraid my sexual desire is inhibited by the urgent need to satisfy the inner man.'

'I'm coming down now,' Sylvia said, all contrition. 'You can have the dried-up Bitkis first then I'll give you tea.'

Over my combined meal Sylvia told me all about the publisher from whom she had received encouragement and also a small advance which she had already paid as a deposit for a pair of contact lenses to replace the hated glasses.

I still felt slightly peeved. 'Why didn't you tell me all this was going on?' I said. 'We used to tell each other everything.'

'You don't realise' – she poured out the tea – 'I hardly ever see you these days. First it was the smallpox, then the snow, now anything and everything. We only seem to say good morning and good night.'

She was right. 'You'd better fix up this Easter holiday thing,' I said, 'to take the children to Paris.'

'I already have.'

'You might have asked me.'

'I did.'

'And what did I say?'

'Yes. Between Mr Nibbs' sciatica and Tommy Knight's croup. Robin says it's all right.'

'What would I do without you?' I put an arm round her hips.

'I see the inner man is satisfied.'

'Fully. Now what about a spot of Dr Linen-bin?'

'His name is Nightshade. Dr Nightshade.'

'I get the idea; "deadly".'

'It's not supposed to be funny!'

I pulled her on to my lap. 'Show me then, in all seriousness, what this admirable practitioner gets up to in his spare time.'

'It isn't even spare. Sometimes he misses most urgent things because of his philandering. There was this patient, you see, very glamorous and quite young, who used to call him in every time her husband went away on business. She'd tell the secretary it was her "usual pain" and that was their code you see for telling him she was available, as it were. So on this particular morning he rushes through the surgery and visits like a knife through butter and finally lands up at this woman's house. He shouts up, "Where are you, darling...?"'

'How did he get in?'

'Don't interrupt. She leaves the door ajar. Where was I...?'

'"Where are you, darling?"'

'Oh yes, he shouts up, "Where are you, darling?" and she shouts down, "In bed, and the pain is absolutely frightful," and he takes the stairs five at a time...'

'Five! It's a physical impossibility.'

'They're very shallow stairs– Anyway, shut up! – and flings open the bedroom door and there she is in one of those mail-order sexy whatnots and he puts down his case...'

'What did he bring it in for?'

'The neighbours, stupid, and hurls himself on to the bed in a wild rush of desire.'

'Go on.'

'Well just then the telephone rings and she holds his hand where it was and says, "Let it ring, Slinky darling." She calls him Slinky. But he says no, because his receptionist is in on all this and knows where to find him. She gets a cuddle too, now and again…'

'He must be enormously virile.'

'Oh he is, enormously. So he answers this telephone, and she says some child's been stung by a bee and could he go? And he says certainly not, not yet at any rate, he frightfully busy – and to tell the mother to put some vinegar on it, or bi-carb, I can never remember which – and puts the phone down. Unfortunately the receptionist, who wasn't as bright as she was cuddly, omitted to tell him the sting was on the child's tongue, and it all swelled up and he nearly suffocated, and it was touch and go while he was merrily dallying.'

'I must say,' I said, 'that I look upon you with new eyes. I never guessed there was such an inventive brain inside that little head of yours.'

'There's a great deal you don't know about me,' Sylvia said darkly, biting my ear affectionately.

Just then the telephone rang. 'Now if I were Dr Deadly Nightshade I'd just ignore it.'

'Well you aren't.' She got off my lap and answered the telephone.

'It's Mrs Purdy. She's just come home from the hospital and she's having trouble with the new baby's feeds.'

'Tell her to ring at surgery time. It's not an emergency.'

Sylvia put her hand over the mouthpiece. 'For your information it is surgery time now!'

I sighed, still not having got round to the morning's visits and took the receiver. 'Yes, Mrs Purdy?'

'I'm having shocking trouble with the baby, Doctor. She's losing weight and not taking her feeds.'

'What are you giving her?'

'Dried milk like they said. They gave me a tin to start me off.'

'How much?'

'Four ounces every four hours.'

'That should be all right. What seems to be the trouble then?'

'Well, Doctor every time she opens her mouth she blows it off the spoon!'

I had been in General Practice too long to laugh, too long even to register surprise.

'Mrs Purdy,' I said slowly and clearly, 'If you read the instructions on the tin you'll see that the milk powder has to be dissolved in water; which mixture you then transfer to a bottle, which your baby will then suck through a teat in which is an appropriately sized hole!'

Mrs Purdy, overcome with my brilliance, thanked me profusely and dashed away to nourish her unfortunate child.

'Well, Mrs Nightshade,' I said to Sylvia...

'Don't call me that!'

'If it really is surgery time I'd better go and freshen myself up while you get on with your secret machinations.'

'With a hungry Cub and Brownie to feed and you no doubt requiring dinner tonight there will be no more time for machinations, secret or otherwise, tonight. And you can stop going on about it and just forgot I told you. We artists are very sensitive.'

'I'll stop on one condition,' I said.

'What's that?'

'That you get one of those mail-order whatsits Slinky's girl friend has.'

'As a matter of fact,' Sylvia said, 'I have.'

I reckoned, going down the stairs, how little one knows about people, even the one knows most intimately. The last thing I could have dreamed Sylvia capable of doing was to write a book. Feeling suddenly inordinately proud of my wife, shortly to be launched as an author, best-seller actually, never mind the contact lenses, I might even retire, I jumped gaily down the last few to collide with Robin in the hall who didn't look the slightest bit gay. I followed him into his surgery bursting to tell him the news about Sylvia but on my oath not to. I hummed a little tune.

'Can't you shut up!' Robin said.

'What's up? Headache?' I took a sample of new headache cure the traveller had left the previous day. 'Take a couple of these. The only thing I can promise is that they won't kill you.'

'I should never have given them to her,' Robin said, ignoring the tablets and sitting at his desk with his head in his hands. 'It was a damned stupid thing to do.'

'What? To who?'

'All those tablets to Lucy … Gunner.'

I suddenly remembered the dramatic events of the morning, relegated to the back of my mind by Margaret Powell's baby.

'How is she?'

'She'll be all right this time.'

'Why don't you arrange some ECT? You don't seem to be having much success with her.'

'I'm not am I? I don't fancy ECT for Lucy … Gunner.'

He gave me an odd look.

'Cheer up. It's not like you to take things to heart. She'll be fit as a flea in a couple of days and that old man of hers will be coming for vitamin pills to keep up with her. Is the Hawkins baby all right?'

'Yes. They've kept him in overnight.'

'I'll tell you what I'll do. You're going to the *Messiah* tonight aren't you? I'll look in on Kevin and Lucy Gunner after the surgery. I've nothing much else on.'

There was no reaction from Robin. The waiting-room door was opening and closing with alarming regularity.

'You need a few days off,' I said to Robin, bearing in mind Sylvia's idea to take the children to Paris in the holidays.

To my surprise he looked up. 'Would you mind? I was thinking of a bit of a rest. Not for a couple of weeks yet though.'

'Delighted. I think you must be run down.' There was a bottle on his desk of vitamin syrup. 'Have a swig of this. You'll feel better.'

Robin was obviously taking his psychiatry seriously, it was not like him to be down in the mouth. I winked encouragingly but he ignored it and pressed the buzzer on his desk to summon the first patient.

My own first patient looked familiar yet out of place in his surroundings. He was a smartly dressed young man, well, my age at any rate, his coat had a velvet collar, he carried gloves and a cane and a monocle on a chain round his neck. I immediately thought of the gone old days of Bertie Wooster and looked automatically at his feet for spats, when I realised there was something very familiar about his character, very familiar indeed.

'Good evening,' I said.

'Good evening.' The monocle was screwed into the eye.

I waited. There was silence.

'Come along please. I've a waiting-room full. What's the matter with you?' I knew I had laid myself wide open.

'You're the doctor!' I groaned. 'And all that malarkey!'

I looked up sharply. There was no mistaking that voice.

'Herbert!' I said. 'Herbert Trew, what on earth are you doing here?'

'I came to ask you a favour actually, old chap. Sake of "auld lang syne" and all that nonsense. Shan't keep you from your beastly sneezles and wheezles long. Can't say you've changed since the good old dissecting-room days. Jolly lucky we did that leg together or we'd never have got it done. Nasty old place, never did get used to it.' He wrinkled his nose with disgust and the monocle fell from his eye.

'Did you ever quality?'

'How could you doubt it? Took my time of course, but then Mama was such an angel about supporting me. To come to the point, I've a very select practice in Park Street. Shahs and Sheikhs and whatnot. I've a poppet of a Princess, Indian and all that, and she has to hop back to the old Palace and she's scared stiff of flying. Wants yours truly to go with. Don't know if you've tried to get a locum lately but they're hell's thin upon the ground, all this brain drain stuff. Wondered if you'd look after the old place for me for a couple of weeks…'

I was about to protest. He held up his hand.

'Evenings only. I've found someone to cover until six.'

'But Park Street is miles away. They'd be dead by the time I got there.'

'There's the Emergency Call Service if it's something absolutely too tiresome.' He looked at his nails. 'Five guineas a visit.'

'Well...'

He jumped up. 'I knew you would. Frightfully decent. Must rush. Can always relay on one's old firm.' He was almost at the door.

'Just a moment! Where are you off?'

'To Karachi?' He took a watch from his waistcoat pocket. 'In two hours; must fly! Ha! See you in a couple.'

He was gone and Mrs Brook hobbled in with her arthritis.

After the surgery I gave Miss Nisbet a lift home to her Ronald who would be waiting anxiously for the steak and kidney pie she had left in the automatic oven and drove on to the hospital which had been the scene of the morning's dramas.

Baby Kevin was sleeping peacefully and was no longer in any danger. Lucy Gunner had been moved to the Private Wing.

At first all I could see was flowers, then Harry Gunner looking tired and old in the armchair; finally Lucy, pale but very much alive, in the bed. She was always beautiful. In her flowery bower she was ethereal. She had been crying.

'I have to thank you,' she said.

'I'm glad we were in time.'

'I lost my nerve at the last minute.'

'Don't talk, precious,' Harry Gunner said. 'Try to rest. I'll have a word with the doctor outside.'

Her face was calm, expressionless after the ordeal of the day.

Outside Harry Gunner said, 'Your partner couldn't throw much light on the subject. Lucy has everything she wants; everything. She has nothing in the world to be depressed about.'

'Sometimes people are depressed for no reason at all.'

'There must be something. I'll give you anything if you find out. Lucy is my whole world.'

'I'll do my best, but really your wife is Dr Letchworth's patient.'

He put a hand on my shoulder. 'I know you will. We can't let this happen again. And thank you for coming to see her.' He went back, a tired old man, into the room. I wondered what on earth Lucy saw in him. I smiled at a young and pretty nurse who said, 'Good evening, sir!' I suddenly realised with something of a shock that I was not as young as I used to be myself!

111

Nine

I went to bed late, tired and confused, which seemed to be the rule rather than the exception these days, and with an irritating cough which often troubled me when I began to need a break. I thought with pleasant anticipation of Sylvia's excellent Paris idea for what must have been a full minute and a half, then fell into a deep sleep. I was woken what seemed seconds later by an elbow applied sharply and firmly to my ribs.

'What on earth's the matter?' I said to Sylvia.

'You are driving me mad. It's two o'clock and I haven't had a wink of sleep.'

'What am I supposed to do about it?'

'Stop coughing. Each time I'm about to drop off, you wake me up again. Cough, cough, cough, cough.'

'Thanks for the sympathy!'

'A creative artist has to get sufficient sleep. Take some cough mixture or something.'

'You know I don't believe in medicine; that's only for the patients. Wait a minute though I did have a bottle of codeine linctus in here from Penny's last bout. I'll take a swig of that if you insist.'

'I don't insist but I really have been very tolerant; two hours of lying awake!'

I reached for the bottle on my beside table, threw back my head and swallowed what I guessed must be roughly a table-spoonful of the contents. 'My God!' I yelled, diving out of bed and foaming at the mouth.

'What is it?' Sylvia turned on the light and followed me into the bathroom.

I was green, speechless and regurgitating. She took the bottle from my hand and read the label.

'Good Lord! Oh dear, what shall I do?' She poured a tumbler full of water. 'Drink this.'

I did and clutched my stomach while the bubbles floated round the room. What seemed hours later I sat sick and exhausted on the edge of the bath.

'Well!' I said to Sylvia.

'Well it was hardly my fault.'

'Whose fault was it then?'

'I just left the shampoo out so that I'd re-member to wash the children's hair tomor-row. How was I to know you'd drink it?'

'I left the bottle of codeine linctus there this morning.'

Sylvia hung her head. 'I gave it to Mrs Glossop for her Arthur.'

There was no more to be said. I had rarely felt so diabolical.

'It was *baby* shampoo,' Sylvia said as we

crawled back into bed. 'Guaranteed not to sting if it gets in the eyes.'

I turned my back on her and tried queasily to sleep. The telephone, as it was absolutely bound to, rang.

I bubbled something into the receiver.

'Is that you, lovey-dovey?'

'This is not lovey-dovey and the time is three a.m. Next time you want lovey-dovey in the middle of the night kindly call the right number.'

'But I did. Where's Herbert?'

'Herbert?' I suddenly remembered Herbert Trew; halfway to India. Hadn't wasted much time in getting the telephone transferred to my number.

'This is Doctor Trew's locum.'

'But I want Herbert.'

'He's gone away.'

'He might have told me. After all it's a bit thick...'

I agreed. 'Look here, what's the matter? Is there anything I can do?'

'I'm sure you can. I've got this absolutely frightful pain.'

'Where?'

'In the usual place. How quickly can you get here?'

'You'd better tell me where the pain is first and how severe it is. It may not be necessary for me to come.'

'Herbert always comes.'

'But I'm not Herbert.'

'No, but I'm sure you're awfully sweet. Herbert wouldn't send anyone unless they were absolutely sweet.'

I sighed; the night was almost gone now anyway. 'Give me the address.'

I wrote it down.

'You'll have to watch out for it; it's just a teeny-weeny little mews. You'll hurry, won't you? I can't move a muscle.'

'Who'll open the door then?'

'Oh don't worry about that, Toto will.'

'It sounds like something out of your book,' I said to Sylvia, pulling on my trousers.

'Whassat?'

'I said it's like something out of your book. A young woman with a pain in the "usual place". You must be psychic. Anyway it sounds as if she has a Chinese manservant or something, so there, I presume, the analogy ends.'

Sylvia opened one eye. 'What on earth are you getting dressed for? It's still dark.'

'Oh go back to sleep, you didn't hear a word I said.'

She sighed and hid her head beneath the bedclothes.

She was right about the teeny-weeny mews in a part of London with which I was unfamiliar. I drove up and down, laughed at, I swear, by the ghoul-faced models in the store windows, looking for its teeny-weeny entrance.

I found it finally, no wider than the car and unlit. Angry now in addition to feeling sick still from the shampoo I took my case from the car and slammed the door.

A window was immediately flung open. 'Can't you bloody well keep quiet!'

'No, I bloody well can't!' I was ready for a fight with anyone. 'Which is number two-A?'

'Good grief; she at it again! In the corner over there – enjoy yourself.'

'I happen to be the doctor!' I said with as much dignity as I could muster, a stomach gurgling with shampoo.

'And I'm the Shah of Persia,' the voice said, slamming the window.

I rang the bell of number two-A. There was silence for a moment then footsteps, odd, light, hurried ones coming downstairs. There was some fumbling with the handle, Toto was obviously drunk or sleepy or both, then the door opened just an inch; nothing more. I began to feel there was something sinister, creepy, about this call. I kicked the door open wide but didn't go in; I too had been to the movies. The hallway was quite two by four and empty.

'Toto!' I said.

From behind the door an Alsatian dog appeared, his head on one side.

I stood for a moment thinking of shampoo and if it contained any toxic ingredients liable to play tricks upon the mind. Was it really three o'clock in the morning and I standing in a darkened and unfamiliar mews before a door which had been opened to me by a dog?

'Come! Toto. Come! Good dog,' the voice I had heard on the telephone called. This was no hallucination.

I followed Toto up the narrow staircase; he waited politely for me a few steps ahead each time, then led me to a door and pushed it open with his nose.

It was not Sylvia's book. She wasn't wearing a mail-order whatnot. She wasn't wearing anything at all. She was lying on a circular bed, beneath a mirrored ceiling, on a black furry rug.

'Good Toto!' she said. Then looked at me.

'It was very naughty of Herbert,' she said, 'not to tell mc he was going away.' She obviously didn't think much of me and I would like to have explained that I wasn't exactly at my best after the shampoo. 'I might have died or something.'

'You'll probably die of exposure like that,' I said.

She picked up a diamond necklace from the bedside table and fastened it round her neck. 'I knew I felt naked.'

I stayed near the door.

She beckoned to me. 'There's nothing to be afraid of. I don't bite. Well not very hard anyway.'

117

I stayed where I was. 'What exactly is the trouble, Mrs … er?'

'Du Bery. You can call me Poppy. And it's Miss. Marriage is so tiresome. I mean getting divorced and then married again. Troublesome and expensive so there's no point in starting if you see what I mean.'

I saw what she meant but little else, not knowing quite where to focus my eyes.

'Aren't you going to put your case down?'

'I might need it.'

She stretched lazily. 'What I need, darling, isn't in that teeny-weeny case.'

That was what I was beginning to suspect.

'Miss Du Bery…'

'Poppy!'

'Poppy then. Why exactly did you bring me here?'

'Don't be angry with Poppy. Gay's in Beirut, Pierre's at one of these health places, he really was getting too enormous, it was beyond a joke, Jojo broke his arm playing polo, Freddie's found some beastly little deb, so what else could I do?'

'Go to sleep.'

'I feel too restless. Anyway I haven't any pills.'

'Oh, I can soon fix that!' I said with relief and opened my case. The contents fell upon the floor. Half a dozen exercise books, a skipping rope, some Crunchie papers and a shower of pencil sharpenings. How often had I told the twins not to leave their cases in the hall!

She was rolling around with laughter. Well, partly laughter, anyway.

She dabbed at her eyes. 'You really are rather sweet after all. I knew Herbert wouldn't let me down.' She held out her arms. 'Now don't waste any more time. Come and see to my nasty old pain.'

I picked up the exercise books and the skipping rope, snapping the case shut and leaving the pencil sharpenings on the white carpet. I suddenly had a brain-wave. 'Look here,' I said. 'I don't believe you have a pain at all and I have a very urgent case to see.' I thought wildly. 'An old lady with cardiac asthma.' I aspirated deeply. 'You know, can't get her breath.'

'What are you going to do,' she asked sweetly, 'pop the skipping rope down her larynx?'

I had enough. I opened the door. Toto sat firmly, with a nasty gleam in his eye, out-side, blocking my path to the stairs. I stood hesitantly.

'You can let him go, Toto,' Poppy said reaching for the telephone receiver. 'I never did care for the smell of Johnson's Baby Powder.'

'Shampoo,' I said.

'Shampoo to you, sexy. Hallo? Larry, angel? I didn't wake you, did I...?'

At breakfast-time I wasn't feeling my best. I pushed away the egg Sylvia had cooked for me and sat disconsolately before the black coffee.

Penny, in T-shirt and blue jeans, came in.

'Go away, there's a good girl. Daddy's tired.'

'You've only just got up.'

'I had to go out in the night.'

'Anything interesting?' They loved to hear the gory details.

'A nymphomaniac. Why aren't you at school, anyway?'

'Half-term. Forgotten?'

'Yes. Run away and play with Peter.'

'There's someone waiting to see you in the hall.'

'Why didn't you tell me then?'

'I'm trying to.'

'Who is it?'

'A chicken.'

'Look, Penny' – I was getting angry – 'I'm in no mood for jokes. I told you I was up half the night. Now push off.'

'But there *is* a chicken in the hall.'

I put my head on my hands. 'All right. There is a chicken in the hall.'

Penny stood where she was. 'She wants to see you.'

'Who does?'

'The chicken.'

I got up menacingly. Penny fled into the

hall into which I followed her. There was a chicken in the hall. A yellow, fluffy one about five feet four in a skin-tight yellow outfit complete with beak at her forehead and a dazzling smile.

'Good morning!' she said brightly, in a refeened voice.

I winced.

'I'm an Egg Chick from the Egg Marketing Board. As you know this is Breakfast Fortnight. Did you know that when you wake in the morning your blood-sugar is low – that's why you feel so bad...'

I didn't like to mention that it was the shampoo.

'...and protein not only puts it up but keeps it up all morning. By going to work on an egg you'll be better-tempered all morning...'

I could hear the waiting-room filling up and clenched my fists.

'...find you have improved efficiency and a nicer nature. After a proper breakfast your engine will be just ticking over nicely!'

Mine was nearly boiling over.

'Well that's extremely kind of you' – I walked towards the door – 'and do tell the Egg Marketing Board I appreciate their solicitude.'

She stood still and held up a webbed hand. 'Just a moment. This is promotion work. If you or any of your family is eating an egg for breakfast when I call you win a one-pound Premium Bond!'

'Daddy is,' Penny said.

'Be quiet. I'm not,' I hissed at her.

'Yes he is. In there.'

The chicken walked into the breakfast-room on whose table reposed my un-touched egg.

'Shall we get Daddy to start his egg, then we can give him his Premium Bond?'

I closed my eyes. 'Daddy has no intention of starting his egg and you know what you can do with your Premium Bond...'

'Don't tell me you're a breakfast skim-per...?' she said.

'Tell me,' I advanced menacingly, 'have you ever seen a chicken with its neck wrung?'

The smile faded and the refeened voice with it.

'All right, all right, I'm going.' She sighed and her feathers seemed to droop. 'I'm packing it in today anyway. Have to get up too flipping early and me feet are killing me. S'pose you haven't got a fag by any chance?'

I gave her one. It was the first time I had seen a chicken smoking.

She put an envelope down on the table. 'Here. You might as well have your ruddy Bond, then I can knock off.'

'There's really no necessity,' I said. 'I couldn't eat that egg if you paid me.' A thought struck me. 'Unless I had a lemon too. Then we'd have a nice egg and lemon shampoo.'

I opened the door and the chicken gave me one odd look and scampered down the path as if the big bad wolf was after her.

Penny was pulling at my sleeve.

'What is it now?' I said.

'There's someone on the telephone for you. Mrs Pepperlumps.'

'Look here, I've had enough of you for one day...'

She fled upstairs. The receiver was off the telephone in the hall. I picked it up.

'Hallo.'

'Hallo, is that the doctor? This is Mrs Pepperlumps...'

Ten

There was still over a week to go before Robin's return from holiday and Herbert Trew's from India and I was beginning to wonder if I would survive those seven long days. In addition to the extra, and to say the least of it, peculiar burden added to my load by Herbert Trew, and the fifty per cent of my own patients generally coped most ably with by Robin, my ancillary help had gone droopy on me. Miss Nisbet, the very epitome of punctuality, had taken to turning up late just when the morning was at its busiest with incoming telephone calls, and Sylvia was a dead loss with this book of hers. When she wasn't actually writing like a lunatic whose very life depended on it she walked round in such a dream, cocooned in chapter nine or ten or whichever it happened to be, that she was little use to me as far as the practice or even the home seemed to be concerned. If she took messages at all she was bound to forget some key factor, she who had once been so efficient, she neglected my missing buttons, any attempt at imagination in the kitchen, and judging by the frequency of their dirty faces, her children. When I chided her gently, oh ever so gently, her hackles rose immediately and she showered me with such biting phrases as 'you'll spend the money all right won't you' and 'you can't expect a creative artist to excel at mundane and routine tasks', that I resigned myself to the state of affairs and looked forward to the moment when she would underline *fin* at the end; if indeed it ever was going to be *fin* about which I sometimes had my doubts. Even Mrs Glossop, our daily help and treasure irreplaceable, had never been the same since her unfortunate incarceration in the smallest room in the house from which she seemed never quite to have recovered. It happened needless to say at the most inconvenient of moments. I had just finished the surgery, the twins were at school, Sylvia was out, and Miss Nisbet had asked if she could go early for some mysterious reason she was unwilling to disclose.

I had a long visiting list, at the top of which was a patient of Robin's which seemed to be reasonably urgent.

'I'm just leaving, Mrs Glossop,' I called up the stairs, 'can you cope with the telephone? I'll ring you in about an hour.'

'Just one moment, Doctor,' the voice came from the distance. 'I couldn't quite catch what you said.'

I heard the flush of the cistern and waited.

'Mrs Glossop!'

'Yes, Doctor.'

'You coming down?'

'Well I was, Doctor, but something seems to be wrong with this door.'

'Give it a good push!' I shouted, struggling into my overcoat. 'It often gets stuck.'

'I am, Doctor.'

'Have you unlocked it?'

'Yes, Doctor. The key turned but something seems to have gone wrong with the handle.'

Muttering imprecations I leapt upstairs, and rattled the handle on the lavatory door. The spring seemed to have packed up. I shut my eyes and counted to ten. Mrs Glossop rattled the handle abortively.

'It's no use doing that, Mrs Glossop. The spring's gone.' I suddenly had a bright idea. 'What about the window?'

'What about it, Doctor?'

'Can't you get out that way?'

'Jump to me death?'

'No, no. Haven't we a long ladder?'

'Yes.'

I breathed again. 'That's all right then. I'll run and get it. This is making me extremely late.'

'We lent it to Dr Phoebe.'

'Lent what?'

'The ladder, Doctor. For her loose tile.'

So we had. 'You stay there,' I yelled through

the door superfluously, 'and I'll nip round outside and see if there's a drainpipe.'

There was no drainpipe. Also the window, no more than a fanlight, would not have admitted Tom Thumb.

I looked up and down the street vaguely for a window cleaner, handyman or decorator.

The street was deserted except for a lady walking by sedately with a shopping basket on wheels who seemed not the slightest concerned with my predicament.

Defeated I went upstairs again with a knife. I tried to insert it round the edge of the door where the tongue had stuck. It was impossible.

'You want a hacksaw,' Mrs Glossop said complacently.

'I haven't got a hacksaw, Mrs Glossop.'

'My Arthur has. Very 'andy is Arthur, not like 'is Dad.'

'Where's your Arthur?' I was halfway to the telephone.

'In the Lake District. Had to take his holiday early on account of the staggering.'

I scratched my head. 'What am I going to do? I can't leave you in there, there's no one to answer the telephone.'

'Otherwise I s'pose you would!'

'No. I didn't mean that; that's not at all what I meant, Mrs Glossop, really.'

'Reckon it'll have to be the fire brigade.'

'The fire brigade?'

'That's what they're there for.'

'I thought only for fires.'

'No! They hardly ever get a fire. Not the fire brigade don't. It's people locked in and putting their heads through railings and doorknobs in their mouths; my neighbour's in the auxiliary, not the Coopers – he's got lung trouble from the shrapnel what got left in his lung, can't hardly breathe poor man – the other side, he's a panel-beater really, during the week that is...'

I dialled, nine, nine, nine.

'Emergency!'

'Well this isn't *exactly* an emergency.'

'Which service do you want?'

'Fire Brigade. But do tell them it isn't a fire.'

The fireman who took down the embarrassing details of the predicament seemed not to turn a hair but had some difficulty with the precise address. He said they would come along at once.

I waited, biting my nails at the dining-room window while Mrs Glossop, I presumed, was sitting comfortably. To my utter surprise, scarcely four minutes later, to the accompaniment of ringing bells, the most enormous fire engine I had seen came slewing round the corner. Clinging to various parts of its anatomy were at the very least a dozen firemen, helmeted and carrying hatchets. It stopped outside the house. The street which a few moments before had been deserted became dotted with curious neighbours hurrying like rabbits from their burrows.

'You did get the correct message?' I said to the chief and fiercest looking fireman to whom I opened the front door.

He took a notebook from his breast pocket and thumbed through its grubby pages. 'One personage incarcerated in toilet?'

'Yes, that's right.' I wondered what he was going to do with all those lifts and fire-hoses he had brought.

I led the way up the stairs followed by half a dozen of the crew.

I pointed to the door which housed Mrs Glossop. The chief rattled the handle. 'Spring's gone!'

'I know.'

He licked his pencil and made a laborious entry in his notebook.

'Have to try the winder.'

'The window is too small,' I said patiently. 'It's only a fanlight window.'

He took no notice of me. ''Arry,' he pointed at one of his cohorts. 'Take a look at the outside winder.'

'Arry and his mates filed in their heavy boots down the stairs again. The minutes ticked endlessly by till their return.

'Too small,' 'Arry reported. 'No more'n a fanlight, really.'

'What about a hacksaw blade?' I suggested.

'Not on this door, you wouldn't do it. Not a 'acksaw wouldn't. Don't know why they build 'em like this I don't.'

'What are you going to do then?'

'Sorry, sir, but we'll 'ave to use force. Don't like to use force, we don't, owing to not knowing what damage might ensue, but force we will 'ave to use. Charlie!'

Charlie, all of eighteen stone and ugly enough not to want to meet on a dark night, came forward.

'It's all yours, Charlie.'

'What is the name of the personage?' the chief said.

'Personage?'

'The personage incarcerated.'

'Mrs Glossop.'

'Mrs Glossop,' he called, bending at the knees and shouting through the keyhole as if she were stone deaf. 'H'ime afraid we are goin' to 'ave to use force in order to effect your release. Would you kindly retreat to the furthest possible point from the door.'

'Well there ain't exactly all that much room in 'ere,' Mrs Glossop said, bitingly. 'I s'pose I could hang from the chandyleer!'

Charlie inserted some jemmy-like instrument in roughly the position of the lock plate, heaved his shoulders up like some prize fighter, then hurled himself at the door which gave to his strength like tissue paper, revealing Mrs Glossop cigarette in mouth, standing on the WC.

'Well,' I said thankfully, 'that's that. Tell me how much I owe you for your help. I have to dash off and do my visits.'

'Just a minute, just a minute,' the chief said. 'I shan't keep you hany longer than necessary, sir, happreciating the nature of your work, but there are one or two formalities.' He took out his notebook once more and turned to Mrs Glossop.

'Have you sustained any injury, madam?'

'In what way?'

'On account of your incarceration. Did you "come over" or anything?'

She gave him a scathing look. 'Do I look as if I "come over". Just locked meself in. Wait till I tell my George. Quite exciting reely.'

'Personage unhurt' was entered into the notebook.

'Can I go now?'

The chief ignored me and was examining the door post.

'Minimal damage,' he said and licked his pencil for a fresh onslaught. 'Sorry about that, sir, but it always does a bit o' damage when we has to burst in. Bit o' plastic wood 'ere and 'ere and you're laughing.'

I was nearly crying with exasperation.

'Look, it was very decent of you to come but I must go now. Please let me settle up.'

He looked horrified. 'Not with us you

131

can't, sir. That's a matter for 'Ead Office. We don't touch the money side. You just sign the forms, sir, and you'll be 'earing from 'Ead Office in due course.'

I took out my pen. 'Where are they then?'

'What?'

'The forms?'

'Tiny!' the chief called to the tallest fireman with the wickedest looking hatchet. 'Nip down to the bus and bring us three forms; sharpish, the gent is in a 'urry.'

We retired to the kitchen where the chief pulled a chair to the table and spread out the three forms Tiny had brought in. It was a multi-questioned form in triplicate starting at the top with time of call, name, address, etc., and having gone through reason for call and the success with which the complaint had been dealt with, ended with a space for signature of householder and date of birth.

'Look, let me just sign on the dotted lines and you can fill in the details at your leisure.'

The chief looked horrified. 'Can't do that I can't, sir. It's as much as my job's worth! Got to know what you're signing, 'aven't you, else it ain't worth the paper it's written on. T'aint legal, anyway!'

I'd had enough. I grabbed the forms, scribbled my name at the bottom of each in the appropriate space and replaced them on the table.

'There!' I said triumphantly, and before he could say another word, 'Mrs Glossop, put the kettle on and make these good gentlemen a nice cup of tea.'

Outside the street was anxious. 'No,' I said, 'it wasn't a fire. No there was no damage. No, I couldn't stop, I had an urgent call to do.'

I backed the car almost out of the drive then swore, it wasn't a pleasant oath, and ran back into the kitchen which was so full of cigarette smoke it looked as if we really were a genuine case. I glared my most sinister glare.

'Would one of you mind moving your – fire engine?' I said as calmly as I was able. 'I can't get my car out of the drive!'

The patient who was first on my list was one of Robin's. Because we were in partnership our list was technically shared but what happened in actual fact was that each of us gravitated towards the people who suited our personalities best. We had discovered early on that in order for any treatment to be beneficial the patient not only had to have faith in the doctor, but the doctor to have faith in the patient; a point which I am sure the patients rarely considered. You couldn't, however hard you tried to convince yourself that you could, give the best of yourself as far as advice, treatment, and particularly sympathy was concerned to a patient in whose presence you felt constantly irritated, or whose voice and mannerisms got on your nerves. Robin and I had different methods of working and encouraged patients to ask for one or other of us specifically accordingly. Those who were unable to get around to their complaint until they had had a cosy chat generally beginning, '...it was last Tuesday, no Wednesday. That's right, I know it was Wednesday because our Harry, that's the one we nearly lost of the whooping cough, has extra maths, on a Wednesday...' usually waited to see Robin. My own particular patients liked to state their symptoms, receive as speedy as possible a diagnosis, accept the advice or treatment without having to hear it repeated half a dozen times, and be off about their business. This week, having to cope with Robin's patients, particularly the ones with whom I was temperamentally unsuited to deal, was particularly harassing. Frequently when I had made a diagnosis, explained treatment, and prognosis, and provided a prescription precious further minutes were wasted in the following manner.

'Now you did say the ointment twice a day and the medicine three times, didn't you, Doctor?'

'No. The medicine twice a day and the ointment three times. Anyway the chemist will write the instructions on the labels.'

'And you think the ointment will clear it up?'

'If it doesn't, come back and see us in a week.'

'You haven't prescribed the medicine that brings him out in blotches like when he had tonsillitis?'

'No, this is something quite different.'

'Only if it's red my neighbour down the road gave it to her Diane and she was smothered.'

'I assure you you'll have no trouble with this. There are no side-effects.'

'Should I cover it with anything?'

'Cover what?'

'After the ointment.'

'That shouldn't be necessary.'

'Only sometimes it stains the bedclothes.'

'This is non-staining.'

'And you can never get it off. What about the medicine, Doctor?'

'What about it?'

'Before or after meals?'

'It really doesn't matter. Whenever it's convenient.'

'Only sometimes it makes them queasy and they don't want anything, and if you give it to them after they bring everything up…'

And so on *ad nauseam*. Robin, being more placid, never minded repeating himself a dozen times. Being more impatient I was inclined to become angry at the unnecessary questions and upset the patient.

The patient of Robin's I was on my way to now was a nice woman, a milkman's wife with five children, who had been on our list for years and never been any trouble. She usually went to Robin because he had injected her varicose veins for her, a minor operation he was expert at and for the purpose of which he usually sat the patient on the window-sill.

According to Miss Nisbet's list Mrs Finch, a woman of about fifty, was complaining of a 'splitting headache' and feeling very poorly. We had known her long enough to realise that if she admitted to 'feeling poorly' she really was; she was the type who presented herself in the waiting-room with a high temperature because she didn't want to put us to the trouble of coming out.

The jovial Mrs Finch was in bed when I arrived and not looking one bit jovial. She had gone to bed early last night, she said, with this splitting headache and now she also had pains in her stomach.

I examined her. Then examined her again.

'Mrs Finch,' I said, 'has anything been troubling you recently? Have you noticed any change in yourself?'

'Well I have felt a bit odd lately, to tell you the truth, Doctor, but I fell down some steps at my daughter's and thought it must be the after-effects. It turns you up, you know.'

'Has Dr Letchworth seen you at all?'

'He has been giving me some tablets for the weight. He said it wasn't unusual to put on a bit at my age.'

'When did he last see you?'

'A couple of weeks, I reckon. I'm just about on the last of the pills now, and he generally gives me about a fortnight's.'

Her face became twisted with pain. I put away my stethoscope thoughtfully, removed my jacket, and rolled up my shirtsleeves.

Mrs Finch began to look alarmed.

'Nothing serious is it, Doctor? Never had a day's illness I haven't. My hubby neither; out in all weathers.'

'It depends what you call serious,' I said slowly, not wishing to give her the shock I had myself just received. 'What would you say if I told you, you were about to have a baby?'

'I'd say you were daft! If you'll excuse me. My eldest is twenty-nine, and I've got six grandchildren.' She sat up. 'Where's Dr Letchworth?'

'He's on holiday, I'm afraid. And even if he weren't there's not much he could do about it.'

'But I only saw him a fortnight ago!'

Oh what a laugh I was going to have on

Robin when he came back.

'It's not his fault, Mrs Finch. Yours is a highly unusual case.'

She grimaced once more with pain and lay down.

'Now you come to mention it,' she said, when the pain was gone, 'it does feel a bit like baby pains, but it isn't possible. My daughter, quick, I must get hold of my daughter.'

I pulled back the bedclothes. 'There's no time for that I'm afraid. You aren't on the phone, are you? I'll yell for a neighbour in a moment.'

'You did say a baby, Doctor?' Mrs Finch said wide-eyed.

'A baby, yes, Mrs Finch,' I said, thinking that the rest of the visiting list would have to wait. 'And I don't think it will be very long before it appears.'

'Whatever will my daughters say,' Mrs Finch said, 'and Tom? He'll pass out!'

We had no time for further speculation. Mrs Finch cried out in pain!

Eleven

An hour later, playing midwife and doctor and cursing Robin when I had the time, I delivered Mrs Finch of a male child seeming not to weigh more than a couple of packets of sugar. We had by this time alerted the neighbours whom, after they had recovered from the shock, became most helpful and one of them had gone touring the streets on his motorbike searching for Mr Finch on his milk float.

'Don't fancy his chances,' one of the more officious neighbours sniffed, glancing at the tiny mite.

'I'm not sure that I do myself.' I wrapped him in a shawl one of them had provided. 'Look, scoot down to the telephone box, ring the City hospital, say you're speaking on my behalf and tell them to send the Premature Baby ambulance immediately.'

'Give us a look Doctor,' Mrs Finch said. 'If I had the strength I'd still think you was having me on!'

'*Me* having *you* on!' I showed her her son.

'Me youngest is twenty-one!' she wailed.

Mrs Finch's Tom, older than his wife and almost due for retirement and pension, came

139

into the already crowded room. I was losing my grip of the situation. Everything was most irregular. There shouldn't have been so many people in the room, the baby was too tiny and there was the risk of infection. Apart from the cluster of neighbours there was a mountain of swaddling clothes in the corner they had good-naturedly raked up hurriedly, many of them smelling, at best, of mothballs. I shooed everyone out and asked them to make poor Mrs Finch a cup of tea, not to mention the long-suffering doctor.

'Now what's all this 'ere?' Mrs Finch's Tom said, pushing his way in, still in his striped milkman's apron.

I showed him the baby.

'Whose is that then?'

'Your'n,' Mrs Finch said.

'Give over, Margaret. A joke's a joke. I think everyone's gone barmy. I was just leaving Pennyfeather's eggs, she always has a dozen Tuesday … MINE? You mean you…?' He pointed accusingly at his wife and sat down hurriedly on the bed, taking off his cap and scratching his head. 'YOU hussy!' he said.

'Well whose do you think it is, Tom? The milkman's?'

'You mean … you … me…' He pointed at the swaddle of shawl.

'You might of told me!'

'No one told me.'

'No, but it was you had it.'

'I never knew, Tom; honest.'

Tom looked at me as I was fastening my cuff links and I didn't like the gleam in his eye.

'It wasn't him, Tom. It was Dr Letchworth.' Mrs Finch said hurriedly in my defence.

'And where is Dr Letchworth? You were only at him a fortnight back.'

'Dr Letchworth is on holiday,' I said, and hurried on in his defence. 'It is of course highly unusual in a woman of your wife's age; although not entirely unknown.'

'Did you *feel* nothing, Margaret?'

'Only after I fell down them steps.'

Tom Finch lay down suddenly on the bed next to his wife, his face a peculiar shade of green. I loosened his collar, then yelled down the stairs, 'Anyone got a drop of brandy!'

'There's a nice cup of tea coming up, Doctor!'

The baby had stopped crying. I shut my eyes with relief as I heard the ringing of ambulance bells.

'Robin, come home!' I said under my breath. Nothing else, surely, could happen in one day.

Fortunately it was the practice half-day and there was no evening surgery.

At dinner-time I made a not very valiant attempt at the Irish stew Sylvia had provided. Immediately she was all hackles.

'What's the matter with it?'

141

'Nothing, darling. It's me. I'm tired.'

'*You're* tired! I shopped all the morning, wrote all the afternoon, took Peter about his brace, cooked the dinner. I was just in the middle of a chapter, too... I meant to ask you, who broke the lavatory door?'

'The fire brigade,' I said as calmly and as quietly as I could. 'Amongst the other calamities which were happening today while you, instead of thinking about nothing but that bilge you keep scribbling, should have been keeping an eye on the practice like every other self-respecting doctor's wife, Mrs Glossop managed to get herself locked in the lavatory from which a fire engine with enough hoses to save the Crystal Palace had to release her, and Mrs Finch, with five children and umpteen grandchildren, well on into the menopause, presented us with a baby...'

'A fire engine!' Peter said, his eyes lighting up. 'Tell us, Daddy...'

'A baby!' Sylvia said. 'Mrs Finch! She must be sixty if she's a day.'

'Fifty.'

'How many firemen?'

'Didn't she know?'

'Did they whoosh up on a long ladder and bring Mrs Glossop down in their arms?'

'Who delivered her?'

'Did they have their helmets on?'

'She must have noticed she was getting fat?'

'Did they ring the bells?'

'Is the baby all right?'

'A fire-engine! Can I go up and tell Penny?'

I removed my hands from my ears. 'I thought there was somebody missing. Where is Penny?'

'Writing lines,' Peter said, half-up from the dinner-table.

'What for?'

'Miss Sneep.'

'I said *what* for?'

'Calling her something.'

'What did she call her?'

'A nymphomaniac.'

I put my head in my hands again.

'Well you told us it, Daddy,' Peter said at the door.

'I suppose you told Miss Sneep that too?'

Peter looked injured. 'No! Penny did though!'

'Why don't you have a rest?' Sylvia said when the remains of the Irish stew and the imaginative and colourful apples and oranges that had followed it had been cleared away. 'You seem to have had a hectic time and it is after all your half-day.'

'I didn't think you even noticed how hard I was working, with Robin away and Herbert's work to do, wrapped up in that bloody book of yours.'

Sylvia sighed. 'I am doing my best.'

'To what?'

'To divide my time fairly between my children, my home, my book and my husband.'

'I'm not at all sure that I like the order of that list.'

Suddenly, for the first time in months now I came to think of it, she was all compassion. She came up to me and put her arms round my neck. 'You don't want me to wear these miserable glasses for the rest of my life!'

'Personally, I can't see that it matters.'

'You know why that is?'

'No.'

'You never look at me.'

A thought suddenly struck me. 'Stand up.'

She stood up, by my knees.

'No. Over there.'

She stood by the door and I looked at her, guilt gnawing creepily at my bones. We had married twelve years ago. Sylvia a stunner amongst fashion models, myself a smart GP. She posed; a front cover of Vogue pose, in her apron, the oven cloth in her hand; she had put on weight; her hair was in need of the attentions of a first-class hairdresser for which she no longer had the time, there was a splash of lamb stew on her honey-coloured shoes, ink on the middle finger of her right hand and no powder on her forehead. The glasses, as usual, were halfway down her nose and did nothing to improve the picture.

'Admit you haven't really looked for many

144

years,' Sylvia said accusingly.

'I haven't really looked for many years.'

'I would never make the front cover of *Bunty*.'

'You would never make the front cover of *Bunty*.'

'I am a wreck. A total wreck.'

I sat down. 'It's all my fault. You should never have married me,' I said self-pityingly.

'Shut-up!' she said sharply, instead of agreeing with me.

She leaned against the door with her arms crossed.

'Now you just listen to me. It's not your fault I've got into this mess. It's because of this book which I am DAMNED WELL GOING TO FINISH and while I'm at it I have to let something go. Firstly myself, secondly the house, thirdly the children, fourthly the cooking, fifthly you and the practice. I have almost finished; almost. Until I have, you will have to put up with me as I am, fat, messy and slightly unsavoury, not to mention these hideous glasses...'

'Darling, if I'd known you wanted contact lenses...'

'It's not just that. I've always been used to working ... not at the kitchen sink, I mean. If I'm successful we'll have a cook and I'll get some clothes and we'll have parties and I'll burn the glasses...'

'Take it easy,' I said. 'They may not even

publish it.'

'They've promised! Hey? Who's that?'

Someone was pushing the door against which she was leaning.

'It's me.'

'Who's me?'

'Penny.'

'And what do you want?'

'How do you spell nymphomaniac?'

It took her five minutes of tongue-biting concentration to get the correct lettering onto the paper.

'How is it,' Sylvia said, 'that you've been up there doing the lines for over an hour and you've only just enquired about the spelling?'

Penny looked at her as if she was simple.

'I did five hundred "I's", five hundred "must's", five hundred "not's", five hundred "call's", five hundred "Miss", five hundred "Sneeps", five hundred "a's", and now I've got five hundred "nymphomaniac's" left. What does it mean anyway?'

Sylvia put her arms around me, fat, be-aproned, glasses, oven-clothed and all, with a wicked glint in her eye. 'It means,' she said. I put a hand over her mouth.

'I think you had better ask Miss Sneep,' I said.

'I don't suppose she'll know.'

'Why's that?'

'She didn't know when Wendy Craig asked

her what adultery meant.'

'What did she say?'

'She said it was in the ten command-
ments, like stealing.'

'Well you'd better go and finish the lines
and we'll have a chat about it later.'

'I can't,' Penny said. 'Peter's adulteried my
Biro.'

When she had gone I straightened my tie
after Sylvia's attentions, and sighed.

'You aren't going out?'

'I'd better go and have a look at Mrs
Finch, poor soul, to see if she's got over the
shock, and I haven't had ten minutes for a
chat with Lucy Gunner.'

'In that case, I shall leave the dishes and
finish Chapter Thirty-Five.'

'How long is this *chef d'œuvre?*'

Sylvia removed her apron and ran her
hands through her hair. She really was quite
pretty still. 'Long enough, I hope, to include
a dish-washer!'

At the Finch's all was peace. The neighbours had repaired to their homes to pass
on the gossip over their respective fences
and the midwife had been in to attend to the
new mother. Mrs Finch's three daughters
and one son sat in the bedroom and looked
upon their mother with awe. Mr Finch had
gone down to the local.

'Wait till we tell our Frank in Australia,'
one of the daughters said.

'He'll think we're having him on!'

'I can't hardly believe it myself,' Mrs Finch said. 'Not with the baby in the hospital.'

'He's doing very well,' I assured her, 'and shouldn't have to be in the incubator for more than a couple of weeks.'

There were tears in her eyes. I sat on the bed. 'Tell me what's worrying you, Mrs Finch. I'm sure your daughters here will all stand by you and help to bring him up. I know it's a bit of a strain at your age when you thought you were past this sort of thing.'

She bridled in her best mauve nightdress. 'Strain, nothing,' she said. 'I can still tell them a thing or two. I'm that happy I can't wait to get him home. Makes you feel a bit silly though, not knowing.'

'It's the best way, Mum,' one of the daughters said. 'Think of all that morning sickness and pains here and pains there and feeling it kick... Didn't you ever feel 'im kickin'?'

Mrs Finch looked embarrassed. 'I did once or twice but I thought it was kippers.'

I left them happy enough discussing the day of excitement and made for the private Nursing Home to which they had removed Lucy Gunner after her attempted suicide. There were so many flowers in the room you could scarcely see the patient. When you did, she was slightly pale but beautiful as ever, lying serenely in her bower, gazed on by her adoring husband.

'Would you like me to wait outside?' he said. 'While you have a word with Lucy?'

'If you don't mind.'

Immaculate in his black jacket and striped trousers, carnation in his buttonhole, and old enough to be her father, he kissed his beloved on her brow. 'I shan't be far away.'

He left the room his eyes on her until the last moment.

'He loves you,' I said, putting my case down and sitting on the bed.

She shrugged disinterestedly.

'Dr Letchworth is still away. I thought I'd just come in and see how you were getting on. More of a social visit really, since you have the Consultant Psychiatrist looking after you.'

'How am I getting on? They said I can go home tomorrow.'

'You look fine to me. But then I'm no psychiatrist.'

'Neither is Harry. Poor Harry.'

Her skin was like porcelain. She raised a wrist as though it weighed a ton. A ruby bracelet encircled it.

'I was never poor,' Lucy said. 'Just middle-class. Girls' High School, tennis team, a good secretarial training, enough clothes, a good time, boy friends, various jobs. I was happy except for my hash of a marriage which fortunately didn't last very long. I was happy when I married Harry. I was in love with him. All at once I had everything. Fur coats, I don't know how many; a car, a chauffeur, a beautiful baby, a cottage in the country, winter in Barbados, summer in Scotland, clothes, jewels. I was still happy. One morning I woke up in my beautiful bed, the bedhead was imported especially from France, and there was no meaning in anything any more; not one single thing. It was as though nothing had anything to do with me. I was detached. The child was someone else's. If it cried I had no feeling for it. If Cook threw a tantrum if left me unmoved. If Harry brought home a necklace all I could feel was the coldness of the stones. I thought it would pass. It grew worse. There was nothing to get up for in the morning; no pleasure in anything the day had to offer. Hundreds of women would have given their right arms for a tenth of the things that made up my life. They could have had them willingly. People began to appear stupid, exchanging money for goods, enthusing over clothes, dances, parties, places, lovers, trips, children, success; the more they talked the more detached I became. I felt so sorry for Harry. He tried to take me out to "take my mind off things". I could only sit silently amazed at the enthusiasm which consumed other people; which were sufficiently important to discuss, to enlarge upon, to pick up the telephone, to convey to others and to others and to others. Sometimes we had no dinner because I ordered none. No social life because I spoke to no one; if they called me I refused their invitations, to dine, to dance, to live. I lay on my bed for hours, staring at nothing, thinking of nothing except to wonder how people could go about their futile little lives. I came to see you, do you remember? You sent me to Dr Letchworth. He helped; he and the tablets. There were times when life became tolerable; only just. Times when I thought perhaps it was going to be all right. I was only numb. The feeling would come back. Harry thought it was things I lacked. No day passed without its gift, carefully thought of, beautifully wrapped. The nightgowns melted like clouds in my hands; the jewels might have been pebbles from a beach which did not hurt my toes. Harry himself seemed far away; a little man. A kind little man; meaningless. I endured; and then I could endure no longer. My mind became increasingly obsessed with thoughts of suicide. With the sweet thoughts of having no longer to think, to be. At first I thought a razor blade and I would hang my wrists over the washbasin and watch it fill to the brim with blood. I wasn't brave enough. I tried, but I wasn't sure which vein, how deep a cut, or whether there would be any pain and how long it would take or if someone would perhaps come in. Then I decided; the tablets. Harry'd brought them from the chemist the night before. Nanny was away with the baby. I waited till he'd gone. The house was quiet. There were so many I thought I should be sick taking them.'

She stopped talking.

'What made you telephone me?'

'Such a stupid thing. Harry was bringing guests from Hong Kong for dinner. There were to be avocado pears. I'd bought them the day before but they were too hard. I put them in the airing cupboard to ripen and forgot to tell Cook. I thought of the guests from Hong Kong and nothing with which to start dinner. I had to tell Cook before ... I had to tell her...'

She looked at the rubies disinterestedly encircling her wrist, watching them clinically as they reflected the light.

'Damn the avocados,' she said.

I wished Robin was back.

Twelve

The following morning, amongst the letters concerning Mrs Rake's chest pains thought by my pal Freddie not to be physical or in particular cardiac in origin, and a report on Mr Close's frontal sinuses and antra which he would be pleased to know had trans-illuminated well, there was a detailed statement from the County Council, County Treasurer's Department. It was headed Fire Services Act, Special Services, and read:

To releasing person from locked lavatory due to defective door catch

Wages

3 Firemen for 26 mins each at 6/1d per hour	7s 11d
1 Station Officer for ditto at 8/5d per hour	3s 8d
	11s 7d
C.C's Sup'n & Nat. Ins Contribution 20%	2s 4d
	13s 11d

Vehicles

1 for 8 minutes at 7/9d per hour	1s 0d

Petrol

1 gallon at 4/5d per gallon	4s 5d
	19s 4d
Administration charge 10%	1s 11d
	1 1s 3d

'Mrs Glossop!' I called.

She came in with my coffee. 'Had to wait for the kettle,' she said. 'It's no use you shouting.'

I handed her the missive from the County Council.

'Twenty-six minutes!' she said. 'They got a cheek. Six for letting me out, that was, and twenty for the cuppa tea!'

'The wheels of bureaucracy, Mrs Glossop.'

'I don't know about that but I think they got a nerve. I mean they didn't need to bring them axes to start with.'

I took the letter back. 'They didn't charge for the axes. I'd better get that handle fixed. I couldn't bear to go through all this again.'

'What about me?' Mrs Glossop removed some of the debris from the table. 'It wasn't you what was locked in.'

I noted that payment should be made to the County Treasurer at the given address and cash sent by registered post, and added the document to my overflowing 'in' tray.

This was the day on which I had promised myself that if the practice was not too terribly busy I would make a resolute attack on its contents. Apart from the inevitable bills, letters concerning patients, invitations, both to patients' celebrations and various clinical evenings and refresher courses, threats to disconnect the electricity and cut off the telephone (bless them), clothes catalogues from the stores where we had accounts telling me that summer was a-coming in and I would not want to be caught out without a selection of their go-easy, go-gay, go-dacron cruise attire in which they assured me I would 'start living', there was a half-inch thick questionnaire concerning the state of General Practice, requiring to be filled in by General Practitioners, which I had been meaning to get my teeth into for some time. The idea of the survey was to compare the lot of the English General Practitioner with that of his brother in the United States to which so many of our brains, including those of many of my oldest friends, had already been drained.

The American leaflet described a group practice worked by thirty-five doctors from central premises and caring for a population of 35,000 patients. The premises were new, cost £175,000 (chicken feed) and were rented by the group. The facilities included office and laboratory spaces and radiology units; twenty-five nurses and thirty-five secretaries. It worked like a combined General Practice and Out-Patient Department, all doctors having access to local hospital beds, and it sounded like bliss. In actual fact though, according to the information, all was not gold that glistened. The patients grumbled that even in such a wonderful place they had no real doctor of their own to go to, and they could never get the doctor to do home calls. The doctors complained that they were over-used for trivial complaints and that the patients were over-demanding. This sounded like home from home and as I gathered up the correspondence I thought might be dealt with by Miss Nisbet and made for my own ill-equipped (by American standards) quarters to my similarly hard-done-by patients I determined, come what may, to get down later to the survey, which stated that to give the best service to the patients the family doctor must: … have adequate time for every patient – ha! … and have a working day which leaves him some time for leisure! If the conditions, and there were several pages of them, were met, a harmonious relationship between doctors and patients would be assured!

Mrs Honeycomb sat patiently in front of my desk. I smiled, to establish our harmonious relationship.

'I wanted to thank you, Doctor,' she said, 'for sending me to that lovely surgeon for my gall-bladder.'

Lovely surgeon? It was still early in the morning. Whom had I sent her to? Lovell was in Africa, Fleming recovering from a prostatectomy; O'Brien! I remembered, my old friend and classmate, kisser of the Blarney stone *par excellence*, Toby O'Brien.

'Really lovely, he was,' Mrs Honeycomb said, 'you know how worried I was what with my heart having to have that nasty op…'

She had every reason to be; an incompetent aortic valve could be quite a risk when undergoing major surgery.

'…he was really lovely anyway and I came for my pills and to thank you for sending me to him. I must tell you what he said when they were getting me ready for the op. You know what you feel like when they put on you those horrible white stockings and the nightshirt? Pitter-pat, I was going, honestly, Doctor, pitter-pat, I'm sure they could hear it all down the ward. Anyway in comes Mr O'Brien, I mean that was nice, he didn't to everyone, sat on the bed he did, Nurse was ever so cross because of the sheets, sat on my bed and held my hand. "Mr O'Brien," I said,

"I hope you don't think I'm talking out of turn or anything like that, only I'm that worried having this incomplete heart, and the kiddies and my husband not all that strong, do you think I'm going to be all right?" I never thought I was going to see that ward again, I can tell you, Doctor. Anyway, he was like an angel; an angel from heaven. He held my hand in his and you know what he said? "Mrs Honeycomb," he said, "I want you to promise me not to worry about a thing; you're going to be fine, just fine." "It's my heart that's worrying me," I said, quietly, not wanting the nurses to think I was soft like. Anyway he leaned over to me and he said: "Mrs Honeycomb, I want you to forget every word about that heart of yours. I give you my solemn promise it will last you as long as you live!" Now wasn't that a lovely thing to say, Doctor? I mean, really!'

'It certainly was,' I said, thinking *trust Toby,* 'and now you've come to be signed off?'

'And to bring you this, Doctor. It isn't very much but I know you always leave yours everywhere.' It was a pair of gloves, two sizes too large. I signed her off, thanked her profusely and laid the gloves on the filing cabinet.

Oddly enough, the next patient was my regular supplier of shirts, ties and various sundries, Miss Chalker.

She looked at the gloves. 'I see someone

has been here before me,' she said. 'Ah well, never mind.' She scrabbled in her shopping bag. 'Just a pullover, I thought yellow for the spring, can't be long now, hanky for the breast pocket of your brown and some Turkish delight!'

'You know my weakness, Miss Chalker. Thank you. What can I do for you today?'

'Nothing, thank you, Doctor, just my tablets and I'll be on my way.'

'I'd better take your blood pressure.'

'Well if you insist, Doctor. You know I don't like to waste your time, with so many people really ill.'

They didn't come more considerate than Miss Chalker.

The next ring of my buzzer brought forth Mrs Ampleworth heavily pregnant and carrying her eighteen-months-old baby in its dressing-gown and looking very anxious.

'I popped her round quickly, Doctor,' she said, 'in case it was anything serious.'

'What seems to be the trouble?' The baby gurgled happily.

'My husband got her up and gave her her breakfast this morning before he went to work then put her back into the cot to play. I was having a bit of a lie-in and she wasn't making any noise so I didn't hurry. Anyway when I went in I nearly had a fit. Look at her?'

I looked across the desk and could see

nothing remiss.

'Her little arm, Doctor, look, she can't move it.'

Now she pointed it out I noticed that the baby was holding her right arm in a rigid and rather unnatural position.

'Let me have a look at her.' I stood up.

'It scares you when you hear about polio and all those things. She had her jabs though; Dr Letchworth gave them to her.'

I took the baby from Mrs Ampleworth. She did not protest when I touched the arm but still seemed unable to move it. I laid her on the examination couch by the window and tried to undo her dressing-gown.

'Your husband is very good at tying knots,' I said, cursing quietly at the silk cords which were unravelling instead of untying.

'Cut it if you like, Doctor. It's only a piece of cord.'

I took my large plaster scissors and cut it through. I eased the good arm out of the dressing-gown which had a pink bunny-rabbit on it and sat the baby up to take it from behind her back. She smiled at me happily. For a moment I stood stock still.

'It's serious!' Mrs Ampleworth said.

After a few manipulations I removed the dressing-gown completely and held both the chubby arms above the baby's head, flexing and retracting them.

'She can move it then?'

I handed Mrs Ampleworth her baby and the dressing-gown with the pink rabbit on it.

'Next time your husband gives her her breakfast, ask him not to manacle her arm to her side with the dressing-gown cord.'

'You mean...'

'She was so tightly tied up she couldn't move her arm.'

'I feel so silly.'

'No need to.' I pressed the buzzer. 'Your husband will have his hand in by the time number two comes along!'

A few pale children, some weary old people, a red-hot appendix, umpteen certificates, and half a dozen injections later I was off to do my first visit. I hurtled up the hill, at the summit of which lived Mr Dodge with his shingles, in my customary manner and was forced to draw up sharply halfway by a scarlet sports car stopped slap in the middle of the road. I couldn't go round it as the hill at that particular point in addition to being particularly steep was narrow and there was a large removal van parked on the offside lane of the road. I hooted impatiently but the woman in the red car, blonde, and wearing, as far as I could see, having been tutored by Sylvia, an ocelot coat, appeared to be having trouble with her gears which were making the most obscene noises. Apart from this all was quiet and the trees, I noticed, were beginning to show the first sign of budding. I gave her a few moments to sort herself out after my initial hooting, and used the time to look in my diary to tot up the number of visits I had for that morning and decided, taking into account both geographical considerations and medical priorities, whom I was going to visit next. Knowing women, as I credited myself with doing, I had stopped a good twenty-five yards behind the red car; there was not one I knew who could start off on a steep hill without a certain amount of back-sliding. What I was not prepared for, however, idly flipping over the pages of my diary while the lady in front selected a suitable gear with which to get herself in motion, was a sudden hurtling backwards down the hill of her vehicle gathering momentum as it went and landing fairly and squarely on my bonnet which it sweetly crumpled, at the same time jerking the steering column with some considerable ferocity into my chest.

For a moment all was quiet. Stove-in chest, I thought; at the very least. While I recovered from the not inconsiderable shock to my system, Ocelot Coat, attractive in a 'one who has been around' kind of way, let her endless pale-stockinged legs out of her car, clutched the skins of the hapless animal about her and stuck her head in my open window. 'You poor, poor man,' I anticipated her solicitude, 'are you all right?

Are you quite sure you're all right?'

Her eyes were green, they were not eight inches from my own; a cigarette was in her mouth.

'What the hell do you think you're doing?' she said, trembling with rage.

'Me? Doing?' My voice emerged as a squeak.

'Ninety miles up the hill like that and smack into the back of me? Can't you see there's a speed limit here? Thirty miles an hour! Can't you read? You have no right to be driving.'

I looked round for help. The road, except for the furniture van from which there seemed no signs of life, was deserted.

'Madam,' I said, disconnecting my chest, which was feeling exceedingly sore, from the steering wheel.

'Don't you madam me! My husband, I'll have you know, is a JP. He doesn't think very much of speed hogs; doesn't think very much of them at all. Do you know I might have been killed? There are too many deaths on the road. Far too many. Most of them caused by selfish nincompoops of drivers who are either drunk or in too much of a hurry to get to some damn-fool place too damn-fool fast!'

My head and ribs were aching. I opened my mouth to say something but she stamped her crocodile shoe upon the ground so I shut it again. She waved a pale-gloved hand. 'Look what you've done to my car. My new car. My anniversary present from Victor. Crumpled like a … like a…'

'Madam,' I said slowly, 'I happen to be…'

'I don't care who you f—g well happen to be. You need to read the Highway Code, that's what you need to do. Read and digest it!'

I watched limply as she stumped back to her car, insinuated herself into the driving seat, slammed the door and in what I am convinced was top gear grated her way up the hill into the distance. Wearily, in my diary, I made a note of the registration number.

When she was gone the road became once more quiet as a morgue. Only a bird twittered. I hate women, I said to no one in particular. I hate women.

Owing to the fact that I spent the rest of the morning getting my injured car towed away, and going through the tedious machinations of hiring another pending its return, my visits were not finished until late afternoon and it was evening before I was able to devote any time to the questionnaire concerning General Practice.

I was still bitter and sore in many respects. Bitter at the perfidy of women, in particular the one in the red sports car with more than the cheek of the devil, and sore in respect of my pectoral muscles which were still feeling the impact of the steering wheel and whose skin was already bluish-black with bruises.

Sylvia had been all compassion, fetching my slippers – I think she must have been watching too many television plays – opening a tin of my favourite soup for dinner and keeping the children out of my hair.

'Never mind the children,' I said. 'Just keep the bloody phone from ringing. I feel about as much like going out tonight as climbing Mount Everest.'

I opened the survey.

A STUDY OF GENERAL PRACTICE
1. How long have you been in General Practice?

Thirteen years, I thought, the best years of my life. I could tell them a thing or two. I filled in the allotted space neatly.

That was question one dealt with. The second question consisted of some twenty-six parts; the answers, known as multiple choice, were to be ticked under the headings, *not a problem, a problem but not serious, a fairly serious problem, a very serious problem.* The items varied from *The number of patients you must assume responsibility for* to *Your opportunities to improve medical skills.* I ticked the appropriate boxes gaily; *had I adequate time for leisure? ... incentives for caring for the time-consuming complex case ... having sufficient time to adequately attend your practice.*

165

(If you can spare the time, would you please elaborate on why you feel problems 3, 4 and 5 are especially important.) I could spare the time.

I ticked gaily on. *Do you as a General Practitioner have direct access to any beds where you retain full responsibility for treatment of your patient while in hospital? What proportion of your time is spent providing psychological supportive treatment? How often, on the average, do you get together socially with other practitioners at a club or other meeting place?* Ha!

'Do you know it's eleven-thirty?' Sylvia said.

'I'm just getting to the really meaty bit!'

Listed below are descriptions of patients who often tend to upset doctors. How often do you see each of these kinds of patients?

This time the boxes were headed *Frequently, Sometimes, Seldom, Never.*

A. A patient who insisted that you visited him in his home even though you felt reasonably certain that the visit wasn't really necessary? Sometimes.

B. A patient who threatened to leave your practice? Sometimes, again. Usually for trivia such as refusing to give Mrs A. the slimming pills you had given her friend Mrs B.

C. A bereaved patient who blames you for the death of a relative? This was a nasty one and sometimes happened particularly with cases of malignant disease which it was impossible to diagnose in the early stages. Sometimes.

166

D. A patient who threatened to write to the local Executive Committee to complain about you? Frequently. Fortunately the threats were mainly hot air and rarely implemented.

E. A patient who lacks gratitude although you have conscientiously taken care of him? Seldom. Although there were of course the odd cases for whom one worked extensively yet never received a word of thanks, just as those for whom one did precious little were often persistently grateful.

How often has each of the following happened in your practice in the last month? A. A patient became hostile to you. B. The patient was a hypochondriac. C. You found yourself dealing with family disputes and marital discord.

'Midnight!' Sylvia said, yawning.

'Shan't be long!'

In general how satisfied are you with General Practice? A. Very satisfied. B. Fairly satisfied. C. Not very satisfied. D. Quite dissatisfied. I ticked answer B.

If you had to do it all over again would you become a General Practitioner? A. Yes, certainly. B. Yes, probably. C. No, probably. D. No, certainly.

I raised my pen; the telephone rang.

'A visit,' Sylvia said, 'one of Herbert's.'

I looked at my watch. 'At this hour?' I put a tick in box C none too kindly and heaved my aching body off the chair.

167

Thirteen

Usually I do not mind doing visits on the midnight roads, it was easy to get about with no hindrance from other traffic nor shopping-happy pedestrians crossing and re-crossing the street. Tonight, however, there was murder in my heart as well as aches and pains in every bone in my body following the morning's mishap. Herbert's patient lived some distance away and the husband had rung off, after peremptorily demanding a visit before Sylvia had been able to find out what it was that his wife was complaining of. Absorbed in the 'Survey of General Practice' as I had been, I hadn't realised quite how tired I was, due probably to the shock I had received. It would have been, I decided now, more sensible to have gone to bed early, as Sylvia had suggested, with a couple of aspirins and a whisky, referring all calls for the night to the Emergency Call Service. I considered my answer to the last question I had completed and wondered if I had been completely honest. 'If you had to do it all over again would you become a General Practitioner?'

Irritated by the ever-demanding telephone

I had ticked 'No, probably'. And yet; and yet...

This was not the first survey on the National Health Service. Most, however, were addressed to patients, not doctors, readers of popular magazines, and came out with some extraordinary findings. It was discovered that comparatively few people were interested in health questions outside their own range of experience and the sad conclusion was drawn that most of us were concerned with our own problems rather than those of general concern. In one such survey I had recently studied, many readers made acrid comments from start to finish, outspokenly complaining of lack of human understanding and using words such as 'morons' and 'cattle' as having been applied to themselves as patients with alarming frequency. Some members of the general public thought that all our problems could be solved by a diet of natural foods. One gentleman, having digested an article in a popular Sunday newspaper blaming sugar for the rise in heart disease, had written to say that as he did not already eat cranberries and Brazil nuts since they were thought to be radio-active, few eggs and little butter owing to their cholesterol content, a trace only of milk because of the Strontium 90 content, no bread or potatoes in order to keep his weight down, he wondered, in all humility if, by leaving out sugar as well from his diet, there was a much greater danger of dying of starvation than from one of the much publicised diseases. He added, in a postscript, that in addition, in accordance with medical recommendation, he did not smoke.

Most people felt that surgeries were adequate although one patient wrote to say 'Our previous doctor did not regard us as patients but as pests!' Reception clerks at the family planning clinics were condemned as treating the women as 'over-fertile cows'.

In my own particular field half the readers chose their doctor because he was recommended; few chose at random or because he was particularly near. Many chose deliberately family men who were good with children and had time to discuss problems.

The cries against the hospitals were well known: old-fashioned, dirty, poor food, inhuman nurses, rudeness and tardiness of consultants. The picture was not all black however, and many were willing to offset the unquestioned failings against relief from financial worry. As far as general practitioners were concerned the age when they behaved and were accepted as little tin gods was past. We had perhaps been none too quick to realise that we were living in a changing world with great social and educational advances as well as medical and scientific ones. The public was better educated and informed than ever before. Information put out over the television and in the press about health and disease was mainly sound and more people knew much more about medicine than they had ever done before. They therefore had much greater expectations about the medical care and attention they would receive when they were sick. We had after all, my colleagues and I, to live up to the reputations of Drs Finlay and Kildare. It mattered not that we never watched the programmes; the public knew, and were not slow to tell, what they were 'entitled to'.

I had decided, many years ago, that General Practice was my proper niche within the health machine and my 'No, probably' reply was set down in a fit of momentary pique. Many times and long and loud from my soap-box I declared to anyone willing to give me an ear, in many respects it is much more important to have a sound family doctor than to be seen by top specialists. It is the family doctor who has to look after you and the family through all the years and all the illnesses, whereas the specialist is called in only occasionally. I personally believed the standards of General Practice still, in the majority of cases, to be very high and that the fact that some of the doctors still treated their patients as morons, pests, or hypochondriacs implied a lack of appreciation and understanding on the part of the practitioner.

We had our moans. We should have a reasonable working day without perpetuating the anachronism of late evening surgeries. We should have a five and a half day week and work only forty-six weeks in the year. Locums and Health centres should be provided, in addition to proper ancillary help. This would give every family doctor sufficient time for post-graduate education and leisure. I knew without any doubt however that Mrs X with her impotent husband, her bed-wetting daughter and her eczematous baby were and always would be my challenge, rather than a hospitalised patient, admitted, cured (or not) discharged and never seen again. In General Practice, we worked hard, it was true, but we not only saw the results of our efforts in the babies we watched over the years grow into children and young adults but of the families we had helped over difficult hurdles and the individuals we had assisted to come to terms with lives not always easy.

I resolved that when, and if, I got home that night I would amend my answer to 'Would you become a General Practitioner again?' from 'No, probably', to 'Yes, certainly'.

Herbert Trew's patients certainly lived in some houses. This one, which I had some difficulty in finding, owing to the darkness of the night and the fact that Peter had borrowed my long-beamed torch for his Cubs activities, was a Georgian-style mansion set back some fifty feet from the road with a huge sweep of well-tended carriage drive.

The door was opened by a handsome middle-aged man in a velvet jacket smoking an outsize cigar. He looked at me and my case as though I were a brush salesman.

'Yes?'

I counted to ten as my mother had taught me and replied civilly:

'I believe your wife is ill?'

'Where's Trew?'

'In Karachi.'

'Sophie has no faith in anyone except Herbert.'

I removed my case from the step and made for the car. This was not my day for being trifled with.

'You'd better have a look at her, I suppose,' he called after me. 'She's in a frightful state.'

He closed the door and took my coat, noticing, as I did, by the light of the most enormous chandelier I had seen outside the Odeon, that Sylvia had neglected amongst other things to sew on my button.

I followed him into the study, library or what have you, which was lined with a great many yards of books, destined, I suspected, never to be read.

'What is the matter with your wife?'

I phrased the question badly and shut my eyes praying silently that at this hour of the night, or morning as it now was, he would not reply that it was I who was the doctor.

I might have guessed that he was far too well bred.

'I believe you call it a whitlow! Had 'em before. Hell's painful, I believe.'

I swallowed hard. A whitlow at one o'clock in the morning. I was glad I was not Herbert. Any patient of mine would have bathed it, poulticed it, taken a couple of aspirins, put up with it at any rate and brought it to the surgery in the morning.

'I'd better have a look at it then.'

The staircase was opulent and was, I swear, lined with Tiepolos.

He pushed open a door off the vast landing. 'My wife is in here.' He preceded me into the room and said, 'Trew is in Karachi, my love. He has sent his locum.'

It could have been a ballroom; it was in fact a bedroom. It was a few moments before I located the bed. My eyes travelled past the rose silk curtains, past the dressing-table bedecked with cherubs, past the seemingly endless flank of built-in cupboards with ormolu trim. When they did finally alight upon the king-size divan they stopped, quite still. Meeting them, the lady in the bed was unable to move hers either. Here, at my complete mercy, ocelot coat exchanged for

174

diaphanous bedjacket, was the lady of the scarlet sports car.

I put down my case on the rose-coloured carpet.

'Good evening,' I said, my voice sinister. Dr Jekyll could have done no better. 'I believe you have a whitlow.'

Her eyes not leaving mine she held up a finger on which was a not terribly inflamed boil.

I nodded knowingly, and said with some gravity, 'Yes. Nasty. I'm sure we can fix that for you.'

Opening my case in silence, I produced a syringe, needle and phial of antibiotic, some of which I inadvertently squirted on to the carpet. When I was ready I marched towards the bed.

She looked at her husband just once then raised the sleeve of her bedjacket an inch.

'We'll have you on your side,' I said authoritatively. 'Either buttock will do.'

I must admit she took it like a trojan. A flash of my arm, a bite of her lips and we were quits.

'Are you all right, Sophie?' her husband said. And then to me as I put away my equipment, 'Poor Sophie's had the most frightful day. Some oaf of a driver ran slap into the back of her Sunbeam this morning. She was in quite a state when I got home, poor lamb; now this! Shall you need to see her again?'

'I'll look in tomorrow, if you like,' I said.

'I'd be grateful if you would. Sophie neglects herself. Shall I settle up now...?' His hand was on his wallet.

I waved an airy hand and looked at Sophie. 'I'll send you a bill!'

I wondered, on my way home, where Herbert found his patients. They were certainly the oddest lot I had ever encountered and I had done quite a few locums myself in my time. They were not all stinkingly rich, but most of them were eccentric. I had grown used to doors being opened by persons of indeterminate sex not to mention remote control and Alsatians. I had become immune to listening to stories of deviated love lives I was expected to unravel and was often invited to join in. I no longer noticed the bizarre surroundings in which many of his patients lived. With a practice such as he had gathered together from I know not where, my answer to the General Practitioner question would be 'not on your nelly!' I was thinking in particular of Mrs Carrington and Lady Jones.

Mrs Carrington had an ovarian cyst the size of a grapefruit in undoubted need of removal. Freddie Lonsdale was to do the operation and left the arrangements, since his secretary was on holiday, to me. Naturally there was to be no National Health

Hospital for Mrs Carrington. Having finished a busy morning surgery, double dose, of course, as Robin was still away, and Miss Nisbet once again indisposed, I rang the Regent Clinic, the most expensive in town where she wished to have her operation, and having waited some ten minutes while they made the necessary enquiries, the place as usual bursting at the seams with patients and booked well ahead, I reserved a bed; I was then transferred to the proper floor, which happened to be engaged speaking, for twenty full minutes, so that I could book the theatre for a time convenient for Freddie on the appropriate day. A further fifteen minutes was taken up with finding an acceptable anaesthetist who happened to be free at that time. Already almost an hour gone from my morning I telephoned Mrs Carrington, engaged speaking, of course, for some further ten minutes, to convey to her the arrangements I had made on her behalf. Further precious moments ticked by while she looked for and finally located her diary.

'Right,' I said. 'Are you ready?'

'Quite ready, Doctor. Can you speak up a little, I can't hear you frightfully well.'

'Is that better?' I shouted.

'Much better, Doctor, thank you.'

'Well, Mrs Carrington, I have managed to fix up a bed for you at the Regent Clinic as you requested. You are to go in on March the twelfth, for operation on thirteenth. Dr Costello will be your anaesthetist, he is one of our best...' I could hear her saying something.

'What's that, Mrs Carrington?'

'I said I couldn't possibly have it done on the thirteenth!'

'But you told me any day in March would suit you.'

'Not the thirteenth, Doctor. Any day but the thirteenth. It is quite unlucky and I wouldn't dream of undergoing an operation of any sort on the thirteenth of the month. It is quite out of the question. What did you say, Doctor?'

I'd said nothing at all except under my breath.

Controlling my voice as best I could I said I would call her back if and when I was able to make alternative arrangements. I passed my lunch hour and the best part of the afternoon in telephoning the various personnel once more, cancelling the previous arrangements and fixing bed, theatre and anaesthetist for the end of the month. Finally I called Mrs Carrington and informed her of what I had done.

She thanked me profusely then said: 'There is just one further point, Doctor. I have of course a private room?'

'But of course,' I assured her. At the Regent Clinic there were only private rooms.

'It's a question of the decorations...'

'You need have no worry on that score, Mrs Carrington. In the past twelve months the place has been entirely redecorated from top to bottom, and you will find everything in perfect order.'

'What colour is my room?'

'Colour! I'm afraid I don't know. Is this frightfully important?'

'Frightfully!'

'I'll have a word with Sister,' I said wearily.

Before retiring for the night, and at the earliest opportunity I had available, I called Mrs Carrington.

'Your room at the Clinic,' I said. 'Sister tells me they have all been painted in the colour found most psychologically beneficial to the invalid.'

'And what colour might that be?'

'A very special shade...'

'Of?'

'Green.'

'Quite out of the question,' Mrs Carrington said, 'and most unlucky. I don't know what they can be thinking of. You will have to make arrangements elsewhere.'

Mrs Gundry was the sweetest thing. She had a chronic condition which necessitated a visit and injection every other day. She lived some considerable distance which took me well out of my way, but I did the journey with a reasonably good will because she was so appreciative. She had just moved to a new flat. The door was invariably opened by a butler, which made a change from Alsatians, and I was shown into the drawing-room where Mrs Gundry was usually *tête-à-tête* with some curtain lady surrounded by satins and silks of the most exquisite colour and quality or standing pensively before some new priceless painting hung temporarily for her approval. Her husband, I understood, not long deceased, had been in sanitary fittings and Mrs Gundry was making the best of the years which remained to her by surrounding herself with beautiful possessions bought with the fruits of that philistine commodity. Sometimes it was a miniature I had to admire, occasionally a lamp. She saw to it that I never left without a cup of Earl Grey, to which her late husband, she assured me, had been particularly partial, and a *petit-four.*

As my visits to her flat were so frequent I thought it polite to send a bill to Mrs Gundry before it amounted to any considerable sum as so easily happened with medical fees.

For a week after she must have received it she made no mention of the matter, then one morning, just after the Earl Grey and while I was deliberating whether it would appear greedy to help myself to one more *petit-four* for the road – I couldn't resist the nutty ones – she drew my attention to the matter.

'Your little bill,' she said, fondling a length of velvet, 'for my little pricks.'

'Ah yes,' I said, 'it's generally better not to let it mount up.'

She leaned forward. 'It isn't a question of mounting up,' she said confidentially. 'It is, I must tell you, that I am quite unable to meet it.'

I looked at the paintings on the walls, the ivories, the miniatures, the lamps, the drapes in situ now, the figurines.

'I can see you understand the predicament in which I find myself,' Mrs Gundry said. 'Another little biscuit, Doctor – they're so small?' She extended the plate. 'But as you must know to furnish a place like this in these times costs one the absolute earth!'

Fourteen

Oddly enough, Sophie, Sophie Trilling that was, and I became quite good friends. After our initial two-round encounter from which neither of us emerged wholly victorious a truce was declared. On the morning after she had summoned me so peremptorily to deal with her whitlow she was downstairs, in a blue silk dressing-gown, arranging flowers. Her hair was round her shoulders, not up as it had been when we'd had our *'crise-de-car'* the previous day, and she looked younger, better disposed and softer.

'How's the finger?' I said warily.

She hid it behind her back. 'I dare say it will mend.'

'May I look?'

'Pax then,' she said.

'Pax.'

One more injection was needed. I took my syringe, employed my most painless technique and dressed the finger. She made me a cup of coffee. We sat in the garden-room, a pleasant place with some attempts at painting, at sewing, at modelling in clay.

'About yesterday,' she said.

'Oh please, think nothing of it.'

'I felt like hell and this finger was bitching me.'

'Water under the bridge,' I said, breathing out and feeling the diabolical pain in my ribs and wondering if I should get them X-rayed.

'I get like that sometimes; it's Victor, he drives me mad. The car was for my birthday, you see. I'd been dying for a lynx coat.' She lit a cigarette. 'I suppose it was a sort of Freudian slip; down the hill, I mean, damaging the car.'

'Couldn't you have asked him for a coat?'

She narrowed her eyes and blew out smoke.

'He bought one. The furrier told me. It wasn't for me though. He has a little girl somewhere. Had her for years. Partly my fault. I'm not very good in bed. Not with Victor, that is. He can't forget his Eton boater, so to speak; it's enough to put anyone off.' She looked at me quizzically. 'You don't really understand, do you? Herbert does.' It appeared there was no end to the things with which Herbert was *au fait*. She sat down opposite me and leaned forward. 'When you see a man, of Victor's type, distinguished looking, *soigné*, over-solicitous to his wife; remembering birthdays, anniversaries, opening doors, pulling out chairs, elegant gifts, long-distance calls, nothing too much trouble, you may be sure he has a bit on the side somewhere.' She stubbed out the cigarette, three-quarters untouched. 'When I married Victor I knew nothing. An elegant catch, I thought…' She waved an arm. 'You mustn't feel sorry for me though. I have my own little amusements.' The dressing-gown parted at the neck. She didn't bother to close it. 'I suppose you have a neat little house, a neat little wife, and neat little children.' She made it sound dirty. 'Do you get any fun out of life though? That's what you must live for; fun. One isn't young for too long. You aren't bad looking when you've had a night's sleep.'

Her eyes were green and the day, listed with visits, seemed dull. Unbidden, a decision of the Disciplinary Committee concerning the doctor's professional relationship with the patient which had recently made headlines and had been upheld by the Committee of the Privy Council rang through my head. '…even if she sets her cap at him he must in no way respond or encourage her…' I shook myself mentally and stood up.

'If your finger bothers you any more let me know.'

'You may be sure I will. We're throwing a party at the end of the month. I'll send you an invitation.'

'That's good of you.' Sylvia loved parties.

She lit another cigarette. 'We'll have another little chat.'

184

It was not my day. I was, I suppose, suffering from the after-effects of my injuries. I felt grisly, gave the patients less than their due and was thoroughly out of sorts. Roll on tomorrow, I thought, when Robin would be back and the following day Herbert Trew. I seemed to be covering the same ground two or even three times as the visits came in by dribs and drabs. At six o'clock I imagined the waiting-room packed, tempers getting short, as I hurried to the address of a patient newly moved to the district who wanted to come on my list and who had a bad pain in her chest. This, I grumbled to myself, would not even be a quick in and out visit. New patients, unfamiliar with my rapid methods of work, had to be introduced to it gradually and a little time spent with them in order to create a good impression on the first occasion.

Mrs Langridge had been recommended by her neighbour. She lived in a bungalow with a miniature rockery and dwarfs with red caps in the front garden. She was a plump, middle-aged lady who thanked me politely for coming so promptly, told me she had just moved south from Middlesbrough where she'd still had the same doctor who had brought her into the world (I reckoned he must be getting on) and was sorry to leave if only for that reason as this good gentleman knew her inside and out, if I understood what she meant.

There was a cosy gas fire burning in the bedroom with its chintzy curtains and I stood in front of it, my stethoscope warming behind my back while she told me the history of her chest.

She had just got to the bit where '...well when the Chest Physician saw my X-rays, he said, "Mrs Langridge, this is the most interesting set of pictures I have ever seen"...' when there was a horrible smell of burning.

'Excuse me, Mrs Langridge,' I said, 'but have you left anything on the cooker? I can smell something burning.'

'No, Doctor,' she said. 'There's nothing cooking.' She sniffed. 'But I can quite definitely smell burning.'

I turned round to look at the fire behind me and saw my stethoscope, my new stethoscope which I had been warming so solicitously for Mrs Langridge's chest, blackened and smouldering slowly, in the flames of the gas fire.

I looked at her and she looked at me.

'Not to worry, Doctor,' she said not frightfully convincingly and giving me a sideways glance. 'I usually take big yellow capsules for my chest anyway.'

I left sadly knowing that I would never now, no matter how hard I tried, measure up to the doctor in Middlesbrough.

I should have started the surgery half an

hour ago. I nipped deftly through the traffic, taking corners at speed until I came to the quiet purlieus of my own neighbourhood. I was just driving down a wide road lined with almond trees when a small boy who had been cycling down the road in front of me with a shopping bag dangling from his handle-bars, started to wobble and fell of his bicycle into the road. Fortunately there was no traffic, other than myself, coming either way. He lay still, the bicycle, its wheels whirring, on top of him. I stopped to see if he had hurt himself. His eyes were open and he looked scared; he must have been about nine or ten. 'You all right, sonny?' I said. 'You want to look where you're going.'

I pulled the bicycle off him and to my surprise a knot of people appeared from nowhere. Housewives had come out of houses, business men, homeward bound in bowlers, newspapers beneath their arms, had appeared and gathered round.

'Criminally careless,' a lady, smelling of chips, in a turban, said, 'Knocking down little children.'

'In such a 'urry to get 'ome to the telly they are!'

'I saw you exceeding the speed limit.'

'Get your licence endorsed for this, my man!'

I suddenly realised that they were talking to me.

'I didn't knock the little fellow down,' I said, smiling.

They looked at my car, not five yards away, in the centre of the road.

'Not much you didn't.'

'Bet 'e's 'urt 'is little 'ead.'

'Lucky it wasn't worse!'

'I once saw one under the wheels of a bus. 'Orrible it was!'

I propped the bicycle against the kerb and kneeled down again beside the boy.

'Take your 'ands off 'im!'

'The ambulance will be here in a moment. I dialled it.'

I took no notice; the boy appeared to be a little shaken but unhurt. I took his hands.

'Up you get then!'

'The cheek of it!'

'You leave him alone till the police comes. Might 'ave 'urt 'is little skull.'

'Didn't ought to be in charge of a car.'

Forty minutes late now for surgery. I dusted the boy down.

'Knocked you off your bike, didn't 'e?'

The lad gazed at the speaker, a stout party in slippers with blue pom-poms on the toes.

A police car drew up.

I attempted to get back into my car. Angry hands pulled at my jacket.

'Tryin' to escape, 'e is, Officer! Knocked this little feller down, now 'e's trying to 'op it. I don't know, you don't 'alf meet 'em

188

these days.'

The Officer took out the inevitable little book. 'Sorry to detain you, sir,' he said.

'Look here,' I said, 'I'm a doctor and…'

'Now 'e's making out 'e's a doctor…'

'Just one moment, if you please, madam,' the Officer said.

'Bleeding cheek.'

'It appears from what these people are saying that you ran into the youth and knocked him from his bicycle.'

I said nothing.

'This is in fact what happened?'

I nodded at the small boy, standing bemused in the middle of the crowd. 'I suggest you ask him.'

'Tell me, young man,' the Officer said, 'did this gentleman here knock you off your bicycle with his motor-car?'

The boy's eyes opened wide.

'I told yer!' Chip-turban said triumphantly.

'Madam, please. This gentleman is in a hurry.'

'I bet 'e is an' all!'

'Did he, then, knock you off your bicycle?'

The boy examined his grazed knee, spat on a dirty handkerchief and rubbed at it.

'I was playin' no 'ands and I missed me pedal, please, sir.'

'Then this gentleman, in whose path you were, presumably knocked you down?'

He rubbed at the grazed knee again.

'No, 'e never! 'E picked me up. Can I go, please, sir, me Mum's waiting on the cabbage.'

'You aren't injured in any way?'

'No. Me Mum'll be mad!'

'So will my patients,' I said giving the Officer my card. 'I have to go.'

The Officer opened the car door for me. 'Frightfully sorry, sir, got quite the wrong impression from these people. Shan't detain you any longer.' He touched his cap and I had a boyish urge to put out my tongue at the crowd standing in the road who would if pushed, I was convinced, have lynched me.

Sylvia opened the front door, with tears streaming down her face.

'They're going mad in the waiting-room,' she said. 'Miss Nisbet keep ringing through to see what has happened to you.'

'They'll get short shrift from me tonight,' I said flinging off my coat. 'And what's the matter with you?'

She peered at me through reddened eyes. 'It's my contact lenses. I've been for a fitting and I'm trying them on. I have to keep them in for two hours. It's murder!'

She groped her way to the kitchen and I to the surgery. From the look of things I would be there for hours. Miss Chalker was first. She brought me half a dozen handkerchiefs with my initials on and a septic toe. The next was Margaret Powell, whom I'd seen little of since the birth of her still-born child. She came in smiling.

'Yes, Margaret, what can I do for you?'

'Nothing, Doctor,' she said simpering and holding out her fourth finger on which was a ring with a minute stone. 'Me and Snorty are getting married. I wanted you to sign me passport photers.'

Marriage! I wondered what had happened to the dreams of her name up in lights and China and marrying a lord.

'Congratulations. I'm very pleased to hear it. Very pleased indeed.'

'We've got a room with Snorty's Mum at Wapping, it's ever so near the river which is nice and the shops are handy...'

I recalled her indictment of her own mother busy with the milkman, the supermarket and the Green Shield stamps.

'...and there's a smashing new supermarket just built. Not of course that it will last us for long.'

'What won't?'

'The room with Snorty's Mum.'

'Why's that?'

'Go on. Bet you can guess!'

I sighed. 'Perhaps he'll grow up to be Prime Minister, a pop-singer, a lord or anything...'

'No,' Margaret said, pensive. 'I'd like a little girl really, then...'

'...she can have her name up in lights,' I said.

'That's it. More glamorous like, Snorty says. We're getting married Saturday.'

I signed the passport photographs declaring them to be a genuine likeness of her unprepossessing face.

'Goodbye, Margaret. And I hope you'll be very happy.'

'Ooh I am,' Margaret said. 'It's Snorty, he's changed me way of thinking.'

There was a hooting outside the window.

'Reckon that's Snorty. I do love 'im.'

She walked out in a dream just as Mrs Pertwee came bursting into the consulting room.

'Terribly sorry to interrupt like this, Doctor, but Miss Nisbet has been sick!'

The waiting-room was so crowded I could hardly get through to Miss Nisbet's cubbyhole where she was pea-soup coloured and moaning.

I took her pulse; she was alive.

'I'm going to be sick again.'

'No, please, Miss Nisbet, not here. You must have eaten something for lunch...'

'Ooooh,' Miss Nisbet wailed, 'Ronald said...'

'Look, hang on a minute and I'll get my wife.'

I ran into the house. Sylvia's face was still wet with tears, her eyes reddened.

192

'For God's sake, come and see to the phone and cards,' I said, 'and bring a mop. Miss Nisbet's been sick.'

'I can't see a thing,' Sylvia said, pointing to her eyes. 'And there's still another half an hour to go. Besides which I'm making sauce Hollandaise and it hasn't thickened.'

'Blast the Hollandaise,' I shouted. 'I can't get through that lot on my own!'

Mr Pointer offered to run Miss Nisbet home in his lorry and the red-eyed Sylvia, sniffing prodigiously, attempted ineffectually to find the medical record cards.

I dealt with half a dozen more patients who were quite elated by the drama they had witnessed in my waiting-room and which made up for missing the telly, and dismissing Mr Sidcup with detailed instructions as to how to deal with his athlete's foot I pressed the buzzer for the next patient. No one came in. Since at least twenty-five people had been waiting when last I looked I guessed that the waiting-room could not have been empty. I buzzed again, loudly; again, angrily; again continuously; again angrily. Still I sat in solitary splendour. There was nothing for it but to see for myself what was going on.

The scene which greeted my eyes was fantastic to behold. The patients, to a man, were crawling round the waiting-room on their hands and knees. I put a hand on my head; perhaps my car injury had resulted in some damage to the brain; a hallucination perhaps. Round and round they went running their hands along the floor as they did so.

'Sylvia!' I yelled.

Across a sea of behinds she faced me from Miss Nisbet's cubicle.

'What on earth's going on? Have they all gone mad or have I?'

She wiped her eyes with a piece of the gauze bandage Miss Nisbet kept for keeping the bills, paid and unpaid, letters, answered and unanswered, in order.

'I've lost it,' she said.

'Lost what?'

She pointed to her eye. 'My lens. I sneezed and it just fell out. I must find it. They cost forty pounds a pair and they're on approval.'

I dropped to my hands and knees in the nearest space I could find, feeling every inch of the linoleum with sensitive fingertips.

It was no good. Micro-corneal lenses were no bigger than a little fingernail and almost invisible to the naked eye. It was more than likely that had it once been anywhere on the waiting-room floor someone would by now have trodden on it and crushed it.

I called the room to order; fetched Sylvia's glasses, helped her to transfer the remaining lens to its little box and got back to work.

Much, much later, when Sylvia was cosily

installed in bed, reading the local newspaper, I came wearily into the bedroom. I said: 'I thought you weren't going to get these lenses until you've been paid for this book of yours?'

'Oh, I haven't,' she said. 'You have them on trial but you don't actually have to shell out until you get them. Anyway I'm on the last chapter so I thought I might as well get them fitted. I'll have them in time for the publication party.'

'If you hadn't smashed one to smithereens you might have.'

'It was just unfortunate; me sneezing, I mean. I dare say Mrs Glossop will find it tomorrow when she sweeps. You have to get used to coping with them, the man told me. Anyway it's made my eye feel frightfully queer.'

I removed my tie and sighed, hoping she would be the last patient that night.

'Come nearer to the lamp and let me have a look at it.'

She wriggled across the bed and I raised her eyelid.

'Sylvia!' I said sharply.

'Yes!'

'Is what you were looking for and what you had some twenty-five of my patients down on their hands and knees for, a small, round object concave in shape and slightly tinted?'

'Of course. And I don't suppose I shall ever see it again.'

'It happens to be resting against the cornea beneath your upper lid. If you work it down gently with your finger from the outside of the lid it will centralise itself over the iris from which it may be removed in the orthodox manner.'

'You mean it was stuck up there all the time?'

'All the time.'

'Well would you believe it?'

'Today I would believe anything.'

With the aid of her handbag mirror Sylvia massaged the recalcitrant lens into position, removed it with a snap of her eyelid, caught it expertly in her hand and put it in its little box next to its mate.

She put her glasses on again and snuggled down with the newspaper.

'That's better!' She smiled. 'It was making my eyelid quite sore. How clever you are, honey!'

A moment later she shot up in bed.

'What now?' I said wearily, hanging up my trousers.

'Miss Chalker.'

'What about her?'

'You know all those ties and shirts and hankies and things she gives you?'

'I don't know how I'd maintain my reputation as the best dressed doctor in the vicinity without her.'

'She's been charged with shoplifting!'

'You must be joking!'

'Listen to this.' She cleared her throat. 'Miss Enid Chalker of Nineteen, Penrose Gardens. Charged with stealing a pink nightdress from Roper's.'

'That's her.' I glanced at my tie-rail profusely interspersed with her most acceptable gifts.

'She has asked the magistrate to take *sixty-four* cases of a similar nature into account!'

Fifteen

Robin came back looking fit but his shirt seemed too big around the collar.

'Where have you been?' I said. 'One of those nature-cure places, living on lemon juice with a few colonic irrigations thrown in for good measure?'

'Fishing.'

'Not a pastime I care for.'

'At least one has something to show for it; not like hitting that little ball around mile after mile and ending up either in a filthy temper or too bumptious for words. Not to mention the Post Mortems.' He picked up a stack of letters. 'What's new?'

'Nothing particular. Everything's been hectic. I've been doing Herbert's work as well. Lucy Gunner is maintaining her progress'

'I know.'

'How?'

'I popped round there last night when I got home.'

'You're a bit keen to get back to work, aren't you? Oh yes! You remember Mrs Finch?'

'Twenty-seven Poets Road? Why shouldn't I? What's happened to her? She was all right when I last saw her.'

'When was that?'

'Can't remember exactly. Two or three weeks ago.'

'What were you treating her for?'

'Obesity, if I remember. Menopausal obesity. I think I had her on appetite suppressants. What's all the mystery?'

'No mystery. My faith in you as a diagnostician has simply been shaken. Consideably shaken.'

'For God's sake,' Robin said irritably, 'she was simply a couple of stone overweight and I was trying to reduce her. If anything's happened to her you'd better tell me. It's too early in the morning for games.'

I leaned back in my chair and tapped my hand with a pencil, enjoying the situation.

'Mrs Finch,' I said slowly, 'has given birth to a baby. A male child, weighing four pounds, four ounces, at present at the City hospital in an incubator.'

'Mrs Finch!' Robin said. 'The milkman's wife?'

'Happy Families!' I said. 'It was you who didn't want to play games.'

'If it's a joke I don't think it's very funny.'

'Mr Finch doesn't think it very funny either; I should watch out when he comes to see you. If you need any help, just yell.'

'I can't believe it. I only saw Mrs Finch a few weeks ago.'

'You'll believe it when they bring "Robin" home.'

'Robin! Salt in the wound!' He clapped a hand to his head. 'I suppose I daren't show my face in Poets Road.'

'I shouldn't worry. They've got over the shock now and think it's a huge joke.'

'*They* might do. What else, while we're about it?'

I told him about Miss Nisbet's indisposition of the previous night, about Sylvia's book, and Miss Chalker's sixty-four cases of shoplifting.

For some reason he thought the latter unaccountably funny.

'I can't see anything amusing about it. She's got months inside and I can't even rake up any mitigating circumstances other than a septic toe.'

Robin opened a letter and slid it over the dining-room table, where we dealt every morning with the correspondence, to me.

'Victor and Sophie Trilling request the pleasure ... only not mine!'

Good as her word Sophie Trilling had sent Sylvia and me and invitation to her party.

'May as well go,' I said, then I read the small writing in the corner of the invitation card.

'Oh no we shan't!'

'What's up?'

'"Guests are requested to wear masks and

fancy dress suggesting some historical character." Fancy dress! Some people have nothing better to think of. She can cross us off her list to start with.'

Sylvia thought differently.

'Sounds great fun,' she said. 'I think Marie-Antoinette or possibly Lady Hamilton'

'You can go by yourself then.'

'Won't you be my Lord Nelson?'

'Certainly not. Black tie or I shall stay at home. I'm not making a fool of myself for anyone.'

'Great minds can afford to make themselves small.'

'Still black tie; sorry.'

'Well, it's not until we get back from Paris, so you still have time to think of something.'

'Can't you take "no" for an answer?'

'No,' Sylvia said. 'I shall write and accept. It sounds gorgeous. After all, we don't go to that many fancy-dress balls, do we?'

I had to admit it. 'Not that many.'

My first patient came in without his Medical Record Envelope. I swore under my breath, hating to be held up.

I called Miss Nisbet through the intercom. There was no reply. I kept flashing; still no reply.

The patient, whom I couldn't recall, was no more than five foot three and had a

201

spaniel-like air about him.

'Where the blazes is Miss Nisbet?'

'You mean Mrs Bottomley.'

'How do you know?'

He hung his hat between his knees and twirled it. 'I'm Mr Bottomley.'

'Oh, you're Miss Nisbet's Ronald!'

'Mrs Bottomley.'

'Mrs Bottomley then.' I sighed. Never had I known such a family for protocol. 'Perhaps you could tell me, in that case, the whereabouts of your wife. I have a busy surgery and she doesn't seem to be here. I simply cannot manage without a receptionist.'

He twirled his hat again.

'I'm afraid you'll have to, Doctor.'

'Why? Is something the matter? If it's a question of wages...' I suddenly remembered Miss Nisbet's indisposition of the previous night.

'Your wife is sick?'

He twirled his hat again. 'I suppose you could call it that. I came to inform you, Doctor, that Mrs Bottomley will no longer be able to carry out her duties for you. She would, of course, have liked to provide you with proper notice, but under the circumstances...'

'What are the circumstances?'

He coughed and went red. 'Mrs Bottomley finds herself in a certain condition.' He said it as though it was the fault of the birds and the bees.

'You mean she's pregnant?'

He nodded.

'Good for her!' I scribbled a prescription. 'Look, give her these, two every night, and she'll be fighting fit in a couple of days.'

'I don't believe you quite understand the situation, Doctor. Mrs Bottomley is carrying a child. Our first child. I intend that she do everything possible to give the little mite a proper start in life. She will have breakfast in bed, which I myself shall prepare before I leave for the office, she will have help with the rough, and she will nap of an afternoon. I can't believe you serious, Doctor, when you suggest a couple of pills and continuing her work here at everybody's beck and call. I would have it on my conscience. Besides which' – he stood up and drew himself up to his full height – 'I forbid it.' He clapped his hat on head. 'And while I am here, Doctor, I feel bound to say that I have never approved of Mrs Bottomley's situation here. I think she has been taken advantage of' – (I gathered he meant the late nights because of the smallpox scare) – 'and required to carry out tasks quite unsuitable for a young lady.' I presumed he meant testing the urines which we had taught her to do and to which she had never raised the slightest objection.

He held out his hand which I shook. He looked surprised.

'I was expecting her insurance cards, duly stamped to date.'

'I'm afraid I don't know where they are. You'll have to ask Miss Nis ... your ... I mean Mrs Bottomley. She deals with that sort of thing.'

'I trust your practice will survive without her.'

'Much better with her.' I smiled appealingly. 'You won't change your mind?'

'Jeopardise the life of a little Bottomley? Never. Good morning to you, Doctor.'

I wished him good morning and the best of luck for his wife and future family.

Thus ended the reign, peaceful and serene, of Miss Nisbet.

Mr Bottomley having departed, leaving me filled with dejection at thoughts of having, after so many years, to find and train a new secretary/receptionist. I pressed the buzzer for the next patient.

After another hectic day my first patient in the examining surgery was Herbert, disgustingly brown, from India.

'I can't say I'm sorry to see you,' I said, unsmiling.

He gave me a great thwack on the back which jerked the monocle from his eye and slapped a wad of notes on my desk and sat down on the patient's chair.

'Cheer up, old sod. It can't be that bad. Herbert's back and my patients thought you were A1. Particularly Clarissa.'

'In the teeny-weeny mews?'

Herbert nodded.

'She didn't get much change out of me.'

'Her bark is worse than her bite. You have to know how to treat her.'

'I'll bet you do!'

'Bit different from the old suburban stuff, what!'

'They're all the same.'

'What are?'

'People.'

'Feeling "one degree under"?' Herbert said taking a syringe from his coat pocket and a phial. 'I got this stuff from a quack in Karachi. They extract it from elephant testicles. It performs miracles.'

'What for?'

'Anything. Anybody. Makes the barren fertile, the depressed manic, the manics depressed, the thin fat, the fat thin, what is it that's troubling you?'

'My secretary's left.'

'Pretty?'

'Nothing like that. A bun in the oven.'

'More life in you than I thought. Not to worry anyway. I have for you the most perfect amanuensis this side of the Thames. Speeds, Typing 65, Shorthand 140; measurements, 38-24-38.' He took out his diary and made a note.

'I shall send her along in the morning.'

'That's awfully good of you, Herbert. How do you know she's free?'

He gave me an odd look. 'She's free. Must dash, and thanks for everything. Anything I can do for you, just let me know. Toodle-pip.'

'Toodle-pip,' I said to the four walls. 'Black-bottom and all that.'

We struggled through with neither secretary nor receptionist, Sylvia refusing, point blank, when I spoke to her over the intercom to come and help. By the end of the surgery time I was boiling over with anger at Sylvia's behaviour, harassed, surrounded with records and letters which someone was going to have to file, and convinced I had given the wrong prescriptions to the wrong people. One never realised how dependent upon a secretary one became. I prayed that Herbert's offering was going to turn up.

I showed the door to Mrs Fairclough, twenty stone and just able to get through it, locked up, and went through to the house to deal with my rebellious wife. There was no smell of dinner in any shape or form but a great noise coming from upstairs.

'Sylvia!'

No reply; the thumping became louder.

'Sylvia!'

I made my weary way up the stairs.

In our bedroom the strangest scene appeared to be taking place bearing resemblance most to a tribal dance. The twins in their pyjamas and Sylvia in a black slip were cavorting round the room, jumping on the bed, twirling each other round and chanting some kind of incantation the words I was just unable to catch. They took no notice of me for some time. My patience was exhausted.

'Shuttup!' I yelled. 'All of you.'

At the sound of his master's voice they collapsed in a heap on the bed, breathing heavily.

'Now,' I said, 'perhaps one of you would be good enough to tell me what is going on in this madhouse.'

They yelled something in unison which again I did not catch.

'Peter,' I said, 'as my oldest son...'

'I'm five minutes older than him,' Penny said.

'...As my oldest son will you kindly tell me calmly and quietly what has happened.'

'Mummy's finished her book.'

'Mummy's finished her book,' Penny said.

'I've finished my book!' Sylvia said, beaming.

I mopped my brow. 'Then let us say Amen! Perhaps we will once again be decently clothed, housed and fed.'

Sylvia sat up. 'There's going to be a sequel,' she said. 'I've started it.'

I joined them on the bed and took Sylvia by the shoulders. 'Congratulations, darling, and all that, it really is splendid, but I'm flaked out from struggling through the surgery with no help and I really would like dinner.'

'Dinner!' She said it as though it were something obscene and looked at her watch. 'My God, I haven't done a single solitary thing. You get carried away writing. I had no idea it was so late. He wasn't stuck off after all, you see, and they all lived happily ever after and it made me cry, I was so excited. It's actually finished and I don't think there's a thing in the larder...'

'Listen, calm down,' I said. 'Just give me a tin of beans and I'll be perfectly happy. Robin's back, so he's on duty now. I'm going to have a peaceful evening and a quiet night. What are you looking at me like that for?'

She was standing stock still and gaping.

'Have you forgotten?'

'What?'

'We're going for coffee at the Overnells'!'

I had forgotten. Probably because I did not want to remember. Of all the duty evenings which were plain purgatory, the Overnells' was the worst.

'You'll have to ring up and say I'm doing a delivery.'

'We did that last time.'

'You aren't feeling well.'

'Time before.'

'Darling, I honestly don't think I can bear with any pretensions to civility an evening at the Overnells'.'

Sylvia had struggled into a housecoat whose belt she tied firmly round her neat little waist.

'I'll open a lovely tin of beans, darling, and make some coffee and you'll feel quite different.'

'I might if it were broiled leg of lamb and a Château Pétrus '59.'

I intercepted the look in her eye. 'All right, all right, I know you can't write and cook simultaneously, but the Overnells tonight are the last straw.'

An hour later, replete with baked beans and burned toast, we stood on the Overnells' well-polished doorstep. If there was one thing I hated more than anything it was GPs evenings. Of all of them Clive and Carrie Overnell's were the worst. Since Clive belonged to our Sunday rota and we had to keep on good terms with them we were bound to accept at least one of their copious invitations in about six. Not that the Overnells were bad. That was the trouble. They were too good. So good in fact that they were dreary. Clive was the GP par excellence and Carrie the perfect wife. That was not all. To the chagrin of the rest of us on the rota Clive not only attended to perfection the needs of his patients, he also did all the baking in the Overnell household, such casual tasks as building in great walls of fitted cupboards in the bedrooms, and was the epitome of politeness.

'If Carrie says "You must have a piece of this chocolate cake, Clive made it!" I'm going straight home,' I said to Sylvia as I rang the bell which produced nauseating suburban chimes.

'Shuttup!' Sylvia hissed. 'They can probably hear you!'

They probably did. Within a second Clive opened the front door and his generous mouth wide.

'How lovely to see you both. So glad you could make it this time. It's ages since we've seen you ... burble ... burble...' He took Sylvia's coat, put it on a hanger, buttoned it and hung it in the hall cupboard, then picked up mine which I had flung on a chair disapprovingly and gave it the same treatment.

In the shabby sitting-room the scene was as usual. The drab wives were arranged on one side of the room and their downtrodden, moaning husbands on the other.

Having been greeted by Carrie in a dress a particularly nasty shade of green which she proudly told us Clive had selected, Sylvia took her place with the wives and I with the men. We had apparently finished with golf and cars, late, owing to our hullabaloo at home, and were round to 'night-calls'.

Clive poured two half glasses of a particularly boring sherry and handed the crisps and peanuts of which one was only able to grab two or three before they were whipped away.

'Personally,' Dr Hotchkiss, who was slightly less of a bore than the others, said, 'I never answer the phone at night. Sally does it and says I'm out.'

'What happens if they ring the door bell?'

'Oh, Sally goes down. That's what doctors' wives are for.'

We all knew from past and identical occasions that Sally Hotchkiss, in addition to her nocturnal duties, also did all her husband's secretarial work, acted as receptionist and frightened into submission the most obstructive patient in addition to rearing four children and a Siamese cat.

'I wouldn't dream of waking Carrie in the night,' Clive said. 'Certainly not to let her go downstairs and answer the door in the middle of the night. Might be a drunk or something.'

'Quite,' Hotchkiss said. 'Can't abide drunks. Sally makes mincemeat of them.'

'I don't know how you manage,' I heard Sylvia say to Sally, 'I have quite enough to do with the house and children. Anyway the patients frighten me. I just can't say he's out if he's in. I go red in the face and it gives me away.'

'It's your duty to protect your husband. Do you know that General Practitioners are three times more susceptible to coronary disease than any other section of the population?'

'It's the way they demand things,' Brenda White said, 'prescriptions and surgery times in the middle of the day and can they put calamine on a spot?'

'Mine are trained,' Sally said. 'It's more than their life's worth to phone outside surgery hours.'

'Sally's trained them,' Hotchkiss said. 'All I have to do is sign the prescriptions.'

'I always feel so sorry for them,' Carrie said, 'I mean if your own child's taken ill you don't always want to wait until the next day. You can understand the late calls.'

'Doesn't do to pamper them and kill your husband,' Sally said firmly.

'That's what I always say.' Hotchkiss drained his sherry glass. 'Let them damn well wait. Particularly the convulsions. I always give it five or ten minutes and the panic's over by the time you get there.'

Dr Hotchkiss had one of the largest practices in the district.

'Brenda never comes near the surgery,' Arthur White said. 'I didn't marry an unpaid help.'

'It's the smell of the urines,' Brenda said. 'Arthur never remembers to pour them down the sink!'

'Sally does that as soon as she's tested them.'

'Tested them!' Dr Smart said from the armchair in which it looked as if he was almost asleep. 'I don't remember the last time I tested a urine.'

'Don't you ask for specimens? What about insurance cases?'

'Oh I ask for them. I must have the largest uncatalogued collection in the British Isles.'

'I'm going to bring the coffee in,' Carrie Overnell said hastily, 'if you two have finished your drinks.'

Sylvia and I drained our glasses guiltily. Clive jumped up for them. 'I'll take them, sweetheart.'

We sat round the dining-room table like a Sunday afternoon tea. There was cods' roe spread on water-biscuits, cherry tartlets and chocolate cake heavy with butter-cream. Carrie clapped her hands while Clive poured the coffee. 'Now do help yourselves, everyone, and you must try a piece of the chocolate cake; Clive made it himself!'

Sixteen

'Another late night for no reason,' I said to Sylvia, turning the key thankfully in our own lock. 'And I promise you that if you let me in for that again...'

'It's awfully difficult, without being rude.'

'You'll have to be rude then. If I had to endure another session of Sergeant-Major Sally and Clive's baking I would do something I might regret. Why is it that when GPs get together ... it's such a bore?'

'People haven't the sense to mix their guests,' Sylvia said. 'It's like having a dinner party and serving *pâté* first, middle and last; nothing to whet the appetite, stimulate and satisfy!'

'We are getting literary!'

Sylvia yawned. 'It's true. If they'd had a business man or two, a couple of artists and a rat-catcher things might have been more lively.'

'They couldn't be much less! Patients, cars, golf! Grumble, moan, grumble.'

I enjoyed discussing cases in a reasonable manner with my colleagues but these dreary quasi-social evenings were too much. No more; I vowed going up the stairs, no more.

214

There was a note, on paper torn from a school exercise book, impaled on to our door handle in Peter's writing. 'Dear Dad, Doctor True phoned to say lervinier will be here at nine tomorrow. Love from Peter.'

Sylvia was looking over my shoulder. 'Who or what is "lervinier"?'

'I can only presume it's our new secretary. Herbert promised to send one.'

The penny dropped. 'Oh,' Sylvia said, 'Lavinia!'

She was undressed and in bed like a flash of lightning, a pile of papers in polythene bags scattered around her.

'Now what are you up to?'

'I'm working out Paris. I thought we'd do the bird market on Sunday morning when we arrive and possibly some sightseeing in the "Bateau Mouche"; the Unesco building in the afternoon, there's a garden designed by Isamu Noguchi that's said to be quite fabulous. Monday of course everything is shut so we might try the Bois and the Eiffel Tower, Tuesday the Jardin des Plantes and the Jardin d'Acclimatation. I might leave you there with the children while I do some shopping…'

I removed my tie. 'I'm exhausted already. Will you kindly bear in mind that we will have the children with us and that we are going for a rest. As far as I'm concerned I shall be quite happy to sit outside with a *café-filtre* and watch the world go by, not caring for their aches, their pains, or their flat fee.'

'It is the children's first time!'

'Do you think they'll remember a damned thing a year from now, except perhaps something they had to eat? They are only eleven you know.'

Sylvia began to gather together her papers. 'You'll be sorry when we get there!'

'Oh don't get huffy! I don't really mean it. But you needn't do all that tonight.'

'We're going on Sunday.'

'It's only Wednesday though.'

'On Friday I'm having lunch with my publisher.'

'Tomorrow?'

'Tomorrow I shall be out all day.'

'Where?'

'I'll tell you when I come back.'

'No dinner again, I suppose. Honestly, darling, you're getting more and more queer. If I'd known when I married you…'

'There was positively nothing in the contract that I recall about answering door bells in the dead of night, filing dreary old letters or testing urines. If that's what you wanted you could always have married Sally!'

'No,' I said. 'I never could stick girls with moustaches.'

At least she was punctual.

At nine o'clock precisely the front door

216

bell rang. I was on my way out to the car for my auroscope.

Her smile nearly knocked me flat on the coconut matting.

She held out a leather-gloved hand. 'Lavinia,' she said. 'Herbert said you wanted me.'

I thought it rather an odd way of putting it. She had auburn hair, West-End cut round a perfect freckled face, wore a skin-tight white suit which showed the cleavage between her breasts, and only her eyes were made up.

It was unfortunate that at that precise moment Sylvia should come downstairs in her oldest dressing-gown, a scarf tied round her head, cream on her face and a duster in her hand. Mrs Glossop's George had a touch of his arthritis and Mrs Glossop had had to stay at home to care for him. Sylvia was giving the house a quick do before she went up to town.

She took one look at Lavinia standing on the step, then walked through into the kitchen, her head held high, like the Emperor in his new clothes.

'I didn't know if you wanted me round this way?' Lavinia said.

'Er...? Oh, I see. Yes, you can come through the house, I'll show you your office. It isn't very large I'm afraid.'

'It'll be large enough.'

I wondered why every remark she made sounded obscene. I led the way into the office. 'I understand your speeds are excellent.'

'Oh yes,' she murmured. 'I'm terribly fast.'

'That's good. I have a stack of letters to dictate when the surgery's finished.'

We had to go through the waiting-room, where the patients' eyes nearly popped out of their heads.

Miss Nisbet's white coat hung on the hook.

'Would you like me in this, Doctor?'

'Just as you like. I don't want you to ruin your suit.'

She was already undoing the buttons of her jacket. 'I always think one looks so much more business like.'

In full view of the patients through the glass panel she took off her jacket revealing a strapless bra and much of what was meant to go in it and wriggled herself into the white nylon overall which she belted so tightly round her waist I thought it not possible that she could breathe.

'Right,' she said, taking a scent atomiser from her handbag and spraying herself. '"Miss Diorling",' she explained. 'My favourite. Where would you like me to begin?'

To my surprise she was amazingly efficient. She had worked for a doctor before and dished out MREs, certificates and prescriptions with remarkable efficiency.

The patients were struck dumb and the voices of the men were at least two decibels higher than normal when they had recovered sufficiently to speak to me. I had never known a surgery where everyone was anxious to be seen last, so delightful did they find the spectacle of Lavinia wiggling her way across the waiting-room on her three-inch heels. This I thought was much more fun than Miss Nisbet and I blessed the happy couple's fertility which the previous day had made me so disgruntled.

The last patient gone and the door locked up, Lavinia and I faced each other.

'Now for the letters,' I said. 'We usually have coffee but I'm afraid the daily help isn't here and my wife's gone up to town for the day.'

'Leave it to me,' she said, disappearing into the house. 'I'm used to unfamiliar kitchens.'

She not only produced coffee for both of us but a plate of florentines which Sylvia was probably keeping for a special occasion to which we both did swift justice.

'Now,' I said when she came back from the kitchen having washed up the cups, 'to work.'

She sat opposite me, all brown-kneed and bosomy, pencil poised.

'Dear Mr Spode,' I started. 'Would be grateful if you would look at Miss Hampton, *aet.* thirty-nine. She has been complaining of headaches and the only physical sign was slight blurring of the left optic disc. I would be pleased to have your opinion. Yours sincerely, etc...'

We ploughed steadily on for an hour. Robin had been at his psychiatric outpatients earlier and was now doing the visits.

At twelve-thirty I suggested Lavinia stopped for lunch. 'I'm tired if you're not,' I said.

She smiled. 'I'm fresh as anything. I could go on for ages.'

'I think that will be all anyway. You've quite a bit of typing there.'

She stood up. 'If I come back at two will that be all right? Herbert wasn't sure about the hours.'

'Fine,' I said. 'Miss Nisbet used to get most of the typing done on Wednesday afternoons. Otherwise only mornings and evenings are necessary. It's only a part-time job.'

She went into the cubicle and removed the overall.

'I don't mind a teeny bit. I'm absolutely free.'

I averted my eyes.

She came out with her jacket on. 'Back at two then. 'Bye.'

She raised a hand and teetered down the waiting-room steps.

I opened the window; there was 'Miss Diorling' everywhere.'

'Smells like a bloody brothel in here,' Robin said, coming in from the visits.

'Wait till you see her. Glamorous and efficient. At least we shall get up to date with some of the correspondence.'

'What's her name?'

'Lavinia.'

'Lavinia what?'

I thought for a moment. 'I don't know.'

I opened a tin of sardines for lunch, in doing so remembering the favourite tag of my old Latin master, *facile dictur, difficile factum*, mopping up oil from the kitchen floor, wishing for once we had a cat, and felt slightly resentful that the estimable Lavinia hadn't offered to stay and cook me a little something. At one-forty-five I went upstairs, washed, combed my hair and applied some of the after-shave Sylvia had given me for Christmas which the adverts promised would turn a He-man into a 'She'-man. I considered changing my tie but decided against it. At two o'clock on the dot the front door bell rang.

A young, fresh-faced man stood on the doorstep. 'Good afternoon, sir, if I may take up just a few moments of your time, I see from the p-p-p-plate you are a doctor and must be a b-b-b-busy man...'

'What is it you want?' I felt in my pocket

221

for half-a-crown.

'I merely want, Doctor, that is if you have a moment at your disposal, a moment, which, I may say, may alter your whole life, to discuss the B-b-b-bible with you.'

'The Bible!'

'The B-b-b-bible; we are calling on every house, you see…'

'I'm terribly sorry but I'm really not interested.'

'That's quite all right, Doctor; please don't think I don't understand…'

I shut the door on his Good-days.

It was two-fifteen, two-thirty, two-forty-five, then three.

The bell rang. Perhaps I had misheard; she had said three o'clock not two.

Robin was on the doorstep. 'Sorry. I forgot my key.'

'I thought you were Lavinia.'

'Do I look like Lavinia?'

'Not particularly.'

'She said she was coming back at two. I spent half the morning dictating.'

Robin looked at his watch. 'You can kiss your hand to her!'

'I don't understand it. Herbert said she was so reliable. Perhaps she's had an accident or something.'

Robin gave me a quizzical look. 'Accident, my … foot!'

I rang Herbert. 'Look, Herbert, this girl

you sent us...?'

'Lavinia? Yes, look, I'm most frightfully sorry, but I have a Persian, in oil in the most enormous way, who had to absolutely dash off and his secretary got her thumb stuck in the "shift-lock". There wasn't a moment and the only person I could think of was Lavinia.'

'But, Herbert, I spent half the morning dictating letters.'

'Can't you get someone else to type them?'

'No I cannot,' I said. 'Anyway, she's taken the notebook with her!' I slammed down the phone, vowing never to speak to Herbert again and trying to remember whether the word he had actually used about Lavinia was reliable.

I spent the rest of the afternoon on the telephone to the Employment Bureaux trying to find a secretary/receptionist.

'I'm not having you off to Paris leaving me with no help whatsoever,' Robin said darkly. 'I can't see why Miss Nisbet can't stay on for a bit longer. Most people work these days until they're nine months; or more.'

'She wouldn't fit into the cubicle. It's not her anyway. It's Ronald. He won't allow it.'

'You should have let me deal with it,' Robin said. 'You don't handle these things properly. You have to use the right approach.'

I handed him Miss Nisbet's address on a

scrap of paper.

'Here you are. Ronald comes home at seven, neither a minute to, nor a minute after. I advise you to wait until he's eaten.'

'Don't teach your grandmother to suck eggs,' Robin said, taking the paper. 'Miss Nisbet will be here in the morning.'

'All those letters,' I wailed.

'Miss Nisbet will do them; calm down.'

'No shorthand, and typing with two fingers!'

'It's served very well till now.'

The telephone rang and I answered it brusquely.

'Mrs Hawkins here, Doctor. Kevin's mother.' I remembered the baby whose life I had saved.'

'Yes, I'm listening.'

'Well, it's Paul this time. He's two. He's come out in horrid great blotches.'

'Has he a temperature?'

'I haven't taken it, Doctor.'

'Well, what's he doing?'

'Riding his kiddy-car in the garden.'

'Bring him to the surgery at six, Mrs Hawkins, and I'll have a look at him.'

'Oh, I don't like to. It might be catching for the other patients.'

'It doesn't sound like it.'

'Anyway I've no one to leave Kevin with.'

'Bring him along. Come early and you won't have to wait.'

'Can't you pop round, Doctor? It'll only take a minute for you to look at it.'

'No, I can't, Mrs Hawkins. If I'd popped round to everyone capable of coming to the surgery I'd have dropped dead years ago. Don't worry about it. Put some calamine lotion on if it itches and see you at six o'clock.'

I had the distinct impression that she slammed the receiver down.

'They'd have your life's blood if they could.'

Robin usually agreed, or disagreed with me. He was staring moodily out of the window.

'Allergy of some sort,' I said to myself. 'Bloody nerve.'

Mrs Hawkins didn't come to the surgery at six with Paul. Mr Hawkins came; alone.

'I understand you refused to come and see my son this afternoon,' he said belligerently. 'Is this correct?'

'Absolutely.'

'You know I can report you to the Executive Council?'

'Mr Hawkins, I have a waiting-room full of people. If you came round merely to make speeches, please make it a short one. Yes, I am quite aware you can report me to the Executive Council. For what, if I might ask?'

'For refusing to visit a sick child.'

'The sick child happened to be playing in the garden on his bicycle. I saw no indication from the history your wife gave me that a visit was indicated.'

'That is quite irrelevant, Doctor, we are paying for your services, paying, may I say, handsomely...' He was a little man with elevators on his heels, inferiority complex, Robin would say.

'Where is Paul, by the way?'

Mr Hawkins eased the back of his collar with one finger.

'My wife called in another doctor who came immediately. Paul is suffering from urticaria,' he said importantly.

'Nettlerash,' I said. 'Something he's eaten, as I thought.'

'That is neither here nor there,' Mr Hawkins said. 'I have brought round our medical cards. If you will kindly sign them in the appropriate place we shall put ourselves under the care of a less busy Medical Practitioner.'

'With the greatest of pleasure.' I scribbled my name illegibly on all the cards, seething inside.

In the filthy temper I saw the remaining patients, and locked up punctually.

In the house Sylvia had prepared steak *au poivre* for dinner, accompanied by salad and *pommes frites*. I ate it in silence.

'Don't you notice anything different?'

Sylvia said, when I had disposed of it.

For the first time I looked at her. The old Sylvia, almost. Her hair was beautifully done, her make-up glamorous, and she wore a new dress and no glasses.

'I'm sorry, sweetie, you look beautiful. You really do.'

'I needn't have bothered. You didn't even notice.'

I put an arm round her. 'Forgive me. Something happened in the surgery to make me angry.'

'Tell me.'

'Just something human. You can sweat your guts out for people, save their lives even, or the lives of their children, I actually did with Kevin Hawkins. They never remember. Do one small thing to upset them however, no matter how trivial, and they never forget.'

'Poor sweetie!' Sylvia took me in her arms.

'I'll get over it. I've been in this game long enough. It's not the first time.' I sniffed behind her ears, her neck.

'That's an awfully familiar smell!'

'I hope not. It's the first time I've worn it. It's for the new glamorous me.'

'"Miss Diorling" isn't it?'

'And how,' Sylvia said, 'would you know?'

Seventeen

I shall never know how Robin managed to
inveigle Miss Nisbet into coming back to
work. All I could get out of him was 'you
just have to know how to handle people';
and Miss Nisbet said, 'Dr Letchworth had a
long talk with Ronald; he's very psychological, you know.' I wasn't sure whether she
meant Robin or Ronald so left it at that, the
remains of 'Miss Diorling' on Miss Nisbet's
overall evoking the image of Lavinia whenever she passed by. For two days we were
back to full strength then on Sunday the
great day was come.

'You're sure you can manage without me?'
I asked Robin, who had kindly come to
drive us to the airport.

He eyed the six suitcases Sylvia had
packed for seven days.

'Suppose I said no!'

I picked up a suitcase. 'Grab hold of that.'
I took one myself and we staggered towards
the car. 'What have you got in here, Sylvia,
bombs?'

She gave me a disdainful look. Having
lunched with her publisher at Claridges and
landed herself with a tidy little advance on

her novel, there was no holding her. 'Perhaps there'll be photographers at the airport,' she said. 'Well-known author flies to Paris. Keep Peter out of the way; you know he always sticks his tongue out the minute he sees a camera.'

'I'm very proud of you, darling, I really am,' I'd said when she returned with her advance. 'Did you tell him you wrote most of it in the bathroom?'

The twins were wild with excitement, never having been either in an aeroplane or abroad.

There were no photographers; just a nasty, cold, damp, misty typical English morning. My idea of sitting at pavement cafés was receding.

'It's just because it's early,' Sylvia said more optimistically than she looked, stamping her feet and holding her coat round her as we queued to board the aircraft. 'It'll probably be quite nice later.'

Peter managed to wriggle himself into a window seat. He immediately tried to work out the intricacies of his safety belt then set to work to read the various booklets the company had provided him with pertaining to the flight.

We began to taxi along the runway, the noise of the jets, warming up, beating against our ear-drums.

Sylvia and I were in the seats across the

gangway. Peter was yelling something at us.

'I can't hear, darling,' Sylvia shouted, 'it's too noisy.'

Peter cupped his hands round his mouth. 'I was just telling you that when you hear a whistle blast for an emergency landing you have to take your dentures out!'

'I don't happen to have any!'

'Well take your shoes off anyhow!'

'Here we go!' I said menacingly. 'Look out of the window. It'll rise quite sharply.'

We sped past the other planes on the ground, faster and faster until quite suddenly we were in the air, looking down onto the airport buildings and the Ariel hotel. We had a final glimpse of the green fields and the dinky-cars on the roads, then we were well and truly in the clouds.

'It's like cotton-wool,' Penny said. 'It's the most exciting thing I've done in my whole life!'

'If you lose a dog in Paris,' Peter yelled across the gangway, 'I can tell you where the dog-pound is...'

'We don't happen to have one with us. What are you reading now?'

'A book about Paris. It tells you everything. If you tear your pants...'

'That will do!' Sylvia said. 'Fill in the green card the stewardess gave you and it will be no time before we're there.'

'She's got black stuff on her eyes,' Penny

said dreamily. 'I think I'll be an air-hostess. What's this brown paper-bag for?'

'Did we *have* to bring them?' I said to Sylvia.

'If you want to pawn something...' Peter read on.

'What's "pawn"?' Penny said across the gangway, 'and why has that lady next to you gone all blue?'

Peter looked. We all looked. She was an elderly lady and her head had flopped back against her seat. She was certainly an odd colour.

I got up quickly and pushed past Sylvia. 'Ring the bell for the stewardess,' I said.

'Oh I have,' Peter said. 'It says "In an Emergency..."'

'Look, shut up for a moment, there's a good chap!'

The woman was unconscious. With the help of the steward and the stewardess we managed to lay her flat in the gangway. I explained that I was a doctor.

The other passengers, having turned curiously for a few moments to see what the commotion was about, settled back in their seats, reading the morning newspapers, drinking coffee or sleeping.

This is all very well, I thought, but I didn't even have any equipment with me.

I examined her and to my horror discovered she had acute cardiac arrest. Her

231

pulse was absent and there were no heart sounds. I got to work with external cardiac massage and mouth to mouth breathing and was tiring considerably when she began to show signs of recovery. I continued with the massage until her colour seemed to improve. We were crossing the French coast before she started to stir and open her eyes. She moved her head and whispered something to the stewardess in French.

The stewardess took her hand and reassured her. I felt the plane bank towards Paris and saw the other passengers fasten their safety belts. The old lady had now fully regained consciousness and we helped her back to her seat. The stewardess brought her some brandy and told me the pilot had radioed for her to be met by ambulance at the airport. She still did not look in very good shape but was out of danger.

'If you want to meet some professional women,' Peter read from his booklet...

He was interrupted by the loudspeaker. 'Ladies and Gentlemen, this is your Captain speaking. In two minutes we will land at Orly Airport; the weather is fine and the ground temperature...'

Self-consciously I regained my seat.

'A good job you were here,' Sylvia said, squeezing my hand.

'She was nearly a gonner,' I said.

There was the slightest of jolts and we

232

were down. Paris in the spring.

The ambulance was waiting and we were asked to remain seated while the old lady was helped out of the aircraft.

When it had disappeared into the distance and the stewardess returned smiling, Penny, Peter, Sylvia and myself and a dozen other passengers out of a full complement made our way through the aircraft to the steps.

'Look,' Sylvia said triumphantly, 'photographers!'

Photographers indeed there were, thick upon the ground.

They ignored our descent.

'What are they waiting for?' I asked an air-hostess.

She smiled a dazzling smile. 'A convention of French doctors,' she said. 'They 'ave been to England for a conference!'

'Doctors!'

'*Mais oui!*'

'You mean all those passengers in there?' I pointed to the aircraft.

She looked at me with pity. 'Doctors, yes,' she said. 'Feefty of them. Now if you will please pass along towards the customs 'ouse.'

The sun was shining. There was nothing I could do but hate my French colleagues for *la belle indifférence* and shrug my shoulders Gallicly.

'Come on' – I gathered my little family

round me – 'we're on holiday!'

The customs men were more interested in Sylvia than her six pieces of luggage. Now that I had time for reflection I could see how pretty she had once again become having had herself done over, brought some new clothes and dispensed with her glasses. I vowed secretly once we returned home to try to lessen her onerous duties of a doctor's wife.

We took the airport bus into town and a taxi to our hotel, a modest but modern and clean one, to which we had been recommended. It was still only nine o'clock in the morning.

'Look, let's not unpack,' I said to Sylvia in our bedroom, 'let's stroll along and get some breakfast in the sunshine. We can do all that after dark.'

The children were next door.

'There's a foot-bath in our bathroom,' Peter said, 'as well as a bath and a wash-basin.'

'And,' Penny said, 'we've got a double bed!'

We strolled along towards the Madeleine in the sun, my cares beginning to lift from me and the practice and the patients receding into the far distance.

There was a nice looking café with tables outside. 'This will do,' I said to Sylvia and we sat down at a table.

I order four *cafés complets* and the waiter

disappeared at top speed.

'What did you ask for, Daddy?' Penny said.

'Breakfast. Aren't you hungry?'

'Starved. But where are we going to have it?'

'Here.' I indicated the table on which the waiter was spreading a fresh white paper cloth.

'In the street!'

'That's right.'

She pointed at all the passers-by, some in their Sunday best.

'With everybody watching?'

'Yes.'

'Well, I think that's disgusting!'

After the initial shock of eating and drinking in the street, they soon began to get the hang of things. They discovered you bought stamps in a tobacconist's and posted your letters in a blue box in the wall. They became adept at taking the numbered bus tickets from the dispensing machines to mark their number in the queue and mentioning the ultimate destination of the underground train even if they wanted to get off en route.

We went to the bird market as Sylvia had planned and marvelled at the *exotiques,* tiny birds in all colours of the rainbow. Peter wanted to buy a canary and Penny a pigeon but agreed when we pointed out that the idea was slightly impractical.

We had an unforgettable week.

We stood in front of *Venus de Milo* and Sylvia forestalled Penny by saying 'I know she hasn't arms, dear.' We climbed the hundreds of steps of the Sacré-Coeur, Penny complaining bitterly that her legs ached and she felt dizzy, and Peter asking if he could ring the second largest bell in Paris, sounded only on festivals and important funerals and which could be heard within a ten-mile radius.

Each morning we set out early, passing the peacock colours of the flower market at the end of our road; each day the sun kindly shone. We saw Paris, which we hadn't visited since our honeymoon, through children's eyes. We took a trip down the Seine on the Bateau Mouche, went to the very top of the Eiffel Tower where Peter wanted to know why all the people in the lift were speaking English and Penny said she felt dizzy again. We had lunch in Montmartre where the children insisted on having themselves excruciatingly sketched for vast numbers of francs; we sailed boats in the Tuileries Gardens, visited the wax-works, voted not half as good as Madame Tussaud's, admired Versailles and picnicked at Malmaison.

Towards the end of the week Sylvia said she was going to leave us for a day as threatened, and Penny, Peter and I visited the Jardin d'Acclimatation. They had a trip on a

236

tiny boat propelled by a water mill, watched the monkeys playing ball, stuffed themselves with candy-floss and waffles and whirled round and round on an aeroplane round-about to the accompaniment of shrieks and shouts from watching parents, *'Marie, monte encore!'*, *'Oh la-la'*, *'Bravooo!'*, *'Boris, attention, hein!'* in addition to the cacophony of brakes, hooters, bells and buzzers enough to deafen the most stalwart. The planes, about the safety of which I had my doubts, slowed down finally, the children dismounted. Penny was promptly sick into the bushes then asked could they see the hall of funny mirrors. This was the big moment of the day. I couldn't get them out of the place as they watched themselves and their respected father become long-legged and pin-headed or gargantuan-headed on matchstick legs. They clung to each other, weak with laughter, the tears were rolling down their faces, they went back for more and more and more. I had a brilliant idea; tea.'

We were back before Sylvia, laden with shopping, who was not amused when I asked if she had also bought another suitcase.

The children were almost asleep standing up so we decided with anticipation to put them to bed with a light supper sent up from the restaurant and to dine on our own for once.

We reserved a table at a famous restaurant

237

in the Place des Vosges.

'What a relief,' Sylvia said, 'no kids.'

I held her hand. 'Honeymoon!'

It was thirty minutes before our first course even appeared.

'Bliss,' Sylvia said, 'we're generally finished, washed up and away in a third of the time at home. We should take more holidays. You're looking far better for yours.'

'And you. It's not much fun for you, I suppose, sometimes; that mad scramble we live in.'

'I never minded at one time. I suppose I'm getting older. If my book's a success I shall have a cook or a maid or something before I turn into a worn-out old hag.'

'That you will never be.'

'Do you realise something? We never get time to sit and talk at home? Just trivia, I mean. It's either me giving you messages or you giving me messages and at night we fall asleep dog-tired.'

'Are you unhappy?'

'No time. Just harassed, occasionally.'

'I will see to it when we get back that you will not be harassed.'

Sylvia smiled. 'Are you considering retirement?'

We strolled home arm in arm through the Paris streets.

'It even has a magic smell,' Sylvia said. 'Glad we came?'

'As usual. You think of all the right things. I haven't given Mrs Finch, or Mrs Hawkins, or the Gunners a thought, perhaps they don't even exist. Just Paris and us.' We kissed under a street lamp like lovers and like lovers went home to bed.

In the morning, with *Le Figaro*, the chambermaid brought a letter which was addressed to us and had been delivered by hand.

I turned it over curiously. 'We don't know anyone here.'

Sylvia yawned. 'It's probably an advert for perfume at a discount or tickets for a dress show.'

It was neither. It was from the old lady who had turned blue in the aeroplane. According to the letter, written in perfect English, she had now recovered completely from her attack, had discovered our address from the airline and in order to show her gratitude would like us all to lunch with her at one of Paris' most famous restaurants on the following day.

'What a nice way to end the holiday,' Sylvia said. 'I ate there once in my modelling days. It's completely fabulous and usually garnished with one or two film stars. The children will be thrilled to bits.'

The children were not thrilled at all by the idea of lunch in a famous restaurant.

Penny wanted to go back to the funny

mirrors and Peter had taken a dislike to the old lady as he didn't like people who had a tendency to turn blue.

When we met her at the appointed time, however, she was wearing a saucy hat and only her eyes were blue. Although she must have been nearing eighty, her skin was that of a woman half her age and she carried herself upright and with dignity. We were received with the dignity of the *noblesse,* introduced, seated, and fussed over with much ado. The *Maître d'hotel* addressed her as Madame la Baronne and I gave what was meant to be a threatening glance to Penny and Peter to mind their P's and Q's.

We lunched off Cod's Roe Pâté, and Sauté of Beef Chasseur. For dessert, Madame, with a wink at the children, suggested the *mousse au chocolat,* and with a bowl which would have served a regiment, topped with Chantilly, was set before them. They looked at it then at each other. The waiter served them enormous portions which they despatched with incredible speed and eyed the bowl again.

'Do you think we can have seconds?' Penny whispered.

I saw Peter kick her. 'Didn't you see on the menu how many francs it was?'

'Daddy's not paying, you clot!'

I tried to engage Madame la Baronne in conversation.

'Help yourselves, children,' she said to them, 'it is there to *it* and is the best *mousse au chocolat* in all Paris. Not only that but in a very few minutes the head waiter tells me you will see the most well-known film star in the world with her husband. They will sit at the table on your right.'

At length, and several times, Madame had thanked me for my attentions to her on the flight. Her heart, she said, was most annoying, and gave her trouble at the very worst times.

'I suppose,' she said once philosophically, 'the poor heart becomes very tired. It has been going, remember, for a long, long time.'

Accompanied by a fanfare of waiters and commis the famous film star swept in, shedding her primrose yellow coat as she did and followed at four paces by her equally famous husband.

Even I felt a thrill at being close to people one was so accustomed to watching on the screen. She had skin like the most perfect porcelain with neither line nor mark.

'I suspect,' Madame la Baronne confided in my ear, 'it must take her at least two hours to complete her *toilette*.'

Her *chignon* was piled high on her head and she read the menu disdainfully and unsmiling. She was however quite, quite beautiful; her husband, unkempt and exceedingly masculine, the perfect foil.

'Do you think we can ask for their autographs?' Penny said, 'or no one will believe me when I get back to school.'

'But of course; that is why they appear in public. To feed their vanity as well as their stomachs.'

She signed the children's menus sourly; he asked them did they come from the States and why weren't they at school? Replete with chocolate mousse and proximity to the famous they could not have been happier.

After a lingering coffee we bade farewell to our hostess, who thanked me once again for saving her life, and left me her card to call her whenever we came to Paris again. I would not have liked to bet on whether she would still be on this earth by the time we came again. We kissed on both cheeks however and parted, she to her apartment in the Avenue Foch and the four of us back to the hotel to collect our baggage.

'The end of a perfect week,' Sylvia said. 'What do you think kids? What did you like best?'

'The funny mirrors,' Penny said starting to laugh again at the thought.

'Spending a penny,' Peter said, 'in the middle of the street.'

We might just as well have taken them to Margate!

Eighteen

Spring slid almost imperceptibly into summer. We had to buy a large size in overalls for Miss Nisbet and Lucy Gunner was becoming more depressed, to Robin's despair, he hated failure; otherwise things ticked over much the same. Patients came and went, died, emigrated and joined the Army. Sylvia lost her contact lenses in the house plants, the car, the bed and the Curzon cinema. Her book was to be published in the autumn and she was writing another, having graduated now the news was out, from the bathroom to the dining-room table.

Midsummer's Day fell on a Sunday. It was the day of the Trillings' fancy-dress party and one which no matter how long I lived I knew I would never forget.

'Look, Sylvia, do we really have to go?' I said, referring to the Trillings' party. 'I am, after all, on duty really.'

'You know quite well Robin's doing tonight for you. He has nothing else to do. Besides, as you know perfectly well, I have my costume.'

'Well, I haven't.'

'That's your own fault and you'll look like a fish out of water. It's simply not sporting of you.'

'Then I am not sporting.'

'I don't see why you can't enter into the spirit of things.'

'It's not the spirits I mind.'

'Stop it. I'm really cross with you.'

'You could always wear my Dalek suit,' Peter said.

'It's supposed to be characters from history!'

'It takes up a bit too much room anyway.'

My gratitude to Sylvia for dragging me off to Paris in the spring had been unbounded. I hadn't realised what the hard winter with its smallpox scare, its snow and fog, had taken out of me. I returned renewed, re-freshed, was pleasant to the patients even when they dropped their bottles of medicine on the way home and had to ring for another prescription, and felt better all round.

Midsummer's Day was a scorcher.

'I shall put my bathing trunks on and lie in the garden,' I announced.

'Thought you were on duty till tonight?' Sylvia was already in her bikini and going down to join the twins sloshing around with a huge bowl of water on the lawn.

'Everyone will be at the seaside or out for the day in weather like this. Couldn't be bet-ter in the South of France,' I said to myself.

I stood naked wondering where Sylvia had cunningly put my summer gear away for the winter when the telephone rang.

'Oh please, Doctor, it's Susan,' a voice I recognised as Mrs Sharp's shouted anxiously at me. 'She was eating a boiled sweet and Jeremy thumped her on the back and she coughed and couldn't get her breath and she's passed out!'

I reckoned I had three or four minutes to dress, get the car out, drive to Cherry Mount and remove the obstruction in little Susan Sharp's larynx before she died from asphyxia. I made a quick decision to dispense with dressing, put on the bathrobe I had just taken off and ran down to get the car. Fortunately it was Sunday and there was little traffic. Horrible thoughts passed through my head of having to establish an airway with a 'stab laryngotomy', by puncturing the membrane between the thyroid and the cricoid cartilages with a knife. I reckoned four minutes had passed since Mrs Sharp's call. To her it must have seemed hours, she was standing at the open front door. Susan was lying on the grass in the garden, cyanosed and unconscious, her brother standing white-faced by her.

'A sweet, you said?'

'A boiled sweet.'

There was one chance. I kneeled beside her and pushed a finger behind her tongue and breathed a sigh of relief as I felt the foreign body. In another moment I had dislodged it and forced it into the oesophagus. After a moment or two of artificial respiration Susan was breathing again, opened her eyes and blinked into the bright sun.

'He hit me!' she said, pointing an accusing finger at her brother. Covered in sweat from the hot bath I had just got out of and anxiety, I stood up.

The Sharps couldn't thank me enough. What would I like? Couldn't they give me a drink?

I excused myself, pointing out that I had better go home and get dressed. I said goodbye to Susan playing on the garden swing, not knowing how near to death she had come.

Five minutes later I was once more standing stark naked looking for my bathing trunks when Sylvia came up for some suntan oil.

'You are taking an age,' she said, fumbling around in the drawer amongst her various bottles. 'Why don't you just put something on and come out? You were standing there like that ten minutes ago. What on earth's the matter with you?'

It was too hot to explain that since she had last seen me I had been out and saved a life. 'I can't find my swimming trunks.'

She opened a drawer in front of me. 'Right in front of your nose! Talk about women messing about.'

Cunningly I had persuaded the Post Office to equip my telephone with an extra long lead. I was therefore able to lie on the garden hammock like a Maharajah and deal with calls at the same time. I set the telephone on the table beside me, covered my stomach with the Sunday newspapers, shouted at Penny and Peter not to make so much noise, heaved a sigh of self-indulgent relief and closed my eyes. They remained closed for less than five minutes when Mrs Valentine, who was a pain in the neck *par excellence,* rang to say that she had finished her slimming pills and could she have another prescription? She thought nothing of disturbing me on a Sunday for this and I thought nothing of telling her to come to the surgery, the proper place for them, on Monday. She was closely followed by Mr Slocombe who wanted to know how many of the proprietary anti-carsick pills he should give his child before they left for Brighton. I asked him if it hadn't got instructions on the packet and he said Yes, but he wanted to be sure. Before I had finished page one of the first newspaper, Mrs Adams rang to say what could she give her 'au pair' for her period pains as she refused to get up and help and the neighbours were coming round for a barbecue lunch. She was closely followed by Mr Worrall who wanted to tell me he had hay-fever and had sneezed fifty-five times.

'Who bloody well invented the telephone!' I shouted, slamming down the receiver.

'Daddy!' Penny said.

'Mr Bloody Bell!' Peter added. 'Would you like me to unplug it for you?' he said helpfully.

'No, I'm on duty.' It rang. 'I can't stand it, what's the matter with everyone today? Hello!' I bellowed. 'Who is it?' It was timid Mrs Payne who was never any bother at all.

'I'm ever so sorry, Doctor,' she whispered, 'knowing it's Sunday and all; but it's the lodger; Mr Pierce. I think he's gone.'

'Gone?'

'Passed away. I just took him up his cup of tea, he likes it late of a Sunday. I got the fright of me life and I'm on me own here. I just come out to phone...'

I removed the newspapers from my stomach and heaved myself out of the hammock. 'Shan't be long,' I said to Sylvia frying in Ambre Solaire. 'Take messages, will you?'

I dressed, it looked like a sunless Sunday for me, and made my way to Mrs Payne's. Everyone seemed to be busy and I collected friendly waves from avid car cleaners and eager gardeners.

'I'm all of a state,' Mrs Payne, in her overalls and slippers, said at the bottom of the stairs. 'I couldn't go up there again.'

'Don't worry, I know the way, you stay down here.'

Mr Pierce, the lodger, was indeed lying dead in bed, the covers nearly to his chin. I sighed. I would have to contact the Coroner's Office as I hadn't seen the patient within the last fortnight, I'd only seen him about twice in fact at all. Mr Pierce, as far as I could remember, was, or rather had been, a waiter in some seedy Soho night-club. He had seen Soho for the last time. He was a youngish man, in his thirties, I supposed. I wondered what he had died from. I had no desire to linger in the room which smelled none too pleasant, neither Mrs Payne nor Mr Pierce being too fastidious. I was about to leave when, for no reason I know of, I decided to pull back the bedclothes. I shut my eyes for a moment with horror at the sight. Mr Pierce was lying stark naked, his throat cut from ear to ear.

'Like a cuppa tea, Doctor?' Mrs Payne said when I had recovered sufficiently to go downstairs. I nodded despite the sight of the unsavoury looking cups. 'Then I'm afraid I have to get in touch with the police!'

They never did discover who 'done' the unfortunate Mr Pierce. I had almost been caught with my pants down though, so to speak, as I had all but left without examining the patient as he was so patently dead.

The Sunday went on as it began; calls and enquiries all day, not to mention those of the police concerning Mr Pierce. I didn't bother to resume my swimming trunks, but sat fully dressed and bad tempered by the telephone, which rang all day into the sunshine.

'I should never have taken up medicine,' I said when Sylvia brought tea out into the garden.

'What would you have done then? Don't eat those sandwiches, they're for the children.'

'I should have been a painter. Slow, quiet, out in the fresh air, no work on Sundays.'

'But you can't paint for toffee-apples.'

'A house-painter! And I'll eat the sandwiches if I want. I work hard enough to pay for the damned Marmite!'

'Aren't you glad we're going to the Trillings'? At least you can knock off at seven and put the phone through to Robin.'

'No, I'm not. I'm tired. I've been hopping up and down like a performing flea all day.'

'Never mind, sweetie,' Sylvia said. 'We'll have a marvellous time. A few drinks and you'll be right as rain: that is, if they let you in with no fancy dress. I'm going to start getting ready.'

At seven-thirty, Marie-Antoinette, grey wig, beauty spot and all, walked slowly down the stairs.

'You'll die of heat in that thing!'

'You are gallant. Is that all you have to say?'

'No. You look gorgeous. And just like

250

Marie-Antoinette.'

'And you look horrible. You haven't even started to change!'

The charge was true. My dinner jacket was one of the old-fashioned ones weighing about a ton and I had absolutely no desire to get into it. I did, however, manage to heave myself up and go upstairs to change.

'I look a proper charlie,' I said to the bathroom, as I combed my hair in the mirror, 'black tie on Midsummer's Day. Who the hell wants to go to the bloody Trillings' bloody party anyway?' My mirror image made no reply.

Robin was downstairs.

'You haven't changed your socks,' Marie-Antoinette said.

I looked. They were brown. 'That can be my fancy dress.'

Marie-Antoinette's eyes filled with tears. 'You're being absolutely beastly today. And you know perfectly well that if you make me cry my mascara will run and I'll rub my eye and lose my lens...'

'Oh no! Not that!' It was far too hot for the crawling round on hands and knees game. 'Anything but that. I'll change my socks.'

I gave Robin all the relevant messages, said good night to the twins who were giggling at their mother, and prepared to leave. Robin said he'd just come to deal with some correspondence in his surgery since he was going to be on duty. I had one foot on the front doorstep when the telephone rang. Robin answered it, while I waited.

He held a hand over the receiver. 'Mr Newbold is having a haematemesis.'

'It's only round the corner from the Trillings'. I'll drop Sylvia off and do that one. There's no point in you going all that way.'

'OK,' Robin said. 'Have a good time.'

I left poor Marie-Antoinette, most ungallantly, to teeter down the Trillings' drive alone as the call was extremely urgent and cut the corners as fast as I dared to get to the Newbolds'.

Mr Newbold was in a very poor state, vomiting blood by the pint, the bedroom looked like the Chamber of Horrors, and elderly Mrs Newbold was busy providing receptacles and wringing her hands. I had a quick look at the patient, gave him an injection of morphia and phoned the emergency ambulance to come quicker than at once with some blood and plasma. I waited till it had come and gone with the old couple in it and not fancying Mr Newbold's chances.

Judging by the number of cars in the Trillings' drive and overflowing a hundred yards or more up and down the road in both directions, and the dance music that filled the night air, the party was in full swing. I felt as much like going to a party after my traumatic day as swinging from the treetops. I only hoped the bar was near.

A manservant opened the door and handed me a black mask which I was only too pleased to put on. 'The ballroom and the bar are downstairs, sir,' he said.

I made my way down the stairs and pushed my way through the air heavy with smoke, and kings and queens and knights and ministers and actors and paramours and jesters towards the far end where I could see the bar. I was stopped beneath the chandelier by Sophie Trilling, whose Queen Elizabeth the First's costume and mask disguised her but whose Turkish cigarette and voice gave her away.

She took both my hands in hers and kissed me. 'How absolutely sweet of you to come, you busy man, and what a masterful idea!' She swung me round. 'Look, darlings! Let me introduce you. Dr Crippen himself!' I looked down with horror at Mr Newbold's blood splattered liberally on my dress shirt.

'It looks so authentic,' Sophie said. 'Honestly, it could be real gore!' From the corner, Marie-Antoinette smiled.

All in all it wasn't a bad party. Once I had got over my bad temper and the alcohol had soothed away the cares of the onerous day I began to enjoy myself. Marie-Antoinette appeared to be busy with Charles the First although they had got their centuries a bit mixed up and I found myself, appropriately enough, the sweetest little Florence Nightingale, with eyes the colour of brandy.

We had a candle-lit supper on the terrace, during which many masked couples wandered off entwined towards the shrubbery, danced, and listened to some filthy jokes told by Sophie Trilling. I was just getting comfortable and closer to little Brandy Eyes in the green-house in which there were real melons growing when the door was opened rudely by Victor Trilling.

'Close it, there's a good chap,' I said, removing my mouth from that of Florence Nightingale, 'think of the melons!'

'The police are here,' Victor said. 'They're asking for you.'

I kissed Florence Nightingale on the nose. 'Sorry, little one, but duty calls.' I guessed it must be about Mr Pierce again. 'Perhaps we shall meet again in the Crimea or something.'

The police officers, two of them, were not however concerned with Mr Pierce. 'Sorry to disturb you, sir,' they said, eyeing the blood on my shirt, 'but there's a patient of yours, a Mr Bull, requiring treatment, and since his wife couldn't get hold of a doctor she got in touch with us.'

'But my partner's on duty. Dr Letchworth. The telephone must be put through to his house.'

'Well, I'm sorry to trouble you, sir, but the

doctor wasn't at home and hasn't been all evening. The patient appears most anxious and is in need of medical attention.'

I extricated Marie-Antoinette from the arms of Charles the First and said we had to leave at once. 'Where on earth has Robin got to?' I said. 'We'd better go and investigate.'

I called in on Mr Bull on the way who was in an insulin coma, and, when he had come round, drove on home to see what was going on.

Dr Letchworth had left soon after us, Mrs Watts, our babysitter, said. He said he was going home, and she hadn't seen him since.

Robin's housekeeper said Dr Letchworth had come round to us at six and hadn't been home since. There had been only the one call from Mrs Bull and she had no idea where Dr Letchworth was.

The surgery, including Robin's room, was in darkness. He said he had been going to catch up with some of his correspondence. I switched the light on in his consulting room. The desk was tidy and he had obviously spent a while with his affairs. On a whim, I pulled back the curtain which concealed his examination couch. Robin was lying on it; dead.

Nineteen

We know nothing about anybody. That I had learned. Had anyone told me that on that humid midsummer's night Robin was going to kill himself I would have called him mad. In films they say he couldn't believe the evidence of his own eyes. I knew what they meant. Robin; Robin the jovial; my partner. It wasn't possible. I had had too much to drink at Sophie's. My eyes and hands told me otherwise; he had been dead for some time. I was considering the possible cause of death when I noticed the notebook in which he kept his visiting list on the floor and a pen in his right hand. I picked up the notebook. At the end of Saturday's visits he had written 'barbiturates, more than enough. Sorry, old thing. Couldn't handle the transference situation. I loved her to distraction, still do, and always will, love her, love her, love her...'

I knew at once that it was Lucy Gunner and cursed myself abortively for my blindness, my stupidity, while ringing, for the second time that night, the police.

It was so desperately easy to be wise after the event. Robin, of course, had not been his customary jovial self lately; hadn't laughed at our mutual jokes, the clangers dropped by the patients. Only now I remembered that the first thing he had done on returning from holiday was to go round to Lucy Gunner's before he was even officially on duty again. How quickly he had rushed to her side when she took the overdose of sleeping drugs.

'Couldn't handle the transference situation.' It was Freud who recognised that the deeply affective involvement of the patient with the therapist was most important in order to effect a cure. In short Lucy imagined herself in love with Robin, which was as it should be, in order to work through her problems, but unhappily Robin had fallen for Lucy which as Robin knew perfectly well was not as it should be at all. Firstly she was a married woman, and secondly and most important of all, she was a patient, and any discovery would have put an end to Robin's career.

The police, with whom I went round to the Gunners', were very gentle with Lucy. Afterwards I talked to her alone in the library of her beautiful house.

'Yes, I know,' she said, 'of course I knew. When doesn't a woman know a man is in love with her?'

'But, Lucy, all psychiatric patients fall in love with their therapists and imagine that the love is returned. It's ridiculous to imagine that the same therapist can love Mrs Brown, whom he sees at two o'clock, Mrs Jones, whom he sees at three o'clock, and Mrs Black who is his patient at four-fifteen. It is only a transference situation you see, so that you may talk to him freely without being judged or blamed.'

Lucy lit a cigarette. 'I don't think you quite understand. Robin and I spent the last week of his holiday together in the country. We knew it was a hopeless situation. There was Harry whom I couldn't leave for all the world; and then, of course, I was Robin's patient. We had a flawless week. It rained every single day. I loved him to distraction, we were perfectly suited. There is a saying that forty days before the creation of a child, a heavenly voice issues forth and proclaims, "The daughter of that one is for this one." That's how it was with Robin and me.'

'I never guessed.'

'You weren't intended to. Harry mustn't know either; not ever.'

How could I tell her, sitting there on the white rug, so beautiful, that agreeing to go away with Robin she had signed his death warrant.

'I'll fix you up with someone else,' I said, 'to continue your treatment.'

She stubbed out her cigarette and the tears rolled with the stub into the ashtray. 'You needn't trouble. Harry and I are going away

258

for a while. I told him I had a wild desire to go to Acapulco.' She started to laugh, hysteria mingling with the tears. 'The funny thing is,' she said, 'I can't stand Mexico!'

Thoughts pinged into my head: 'Please don't cry, you'll soon forget him, you have so much to be happy about.' They were all too banal. I went to the door. 'If there's anything I can do,' I said, 'at any time, please let me know.'

For what was left of the night Sylvia and I clung together speechless, or whispering our sadness about what Robin must have suffered during the past months. 'He never let on,' I said, 'not a sign.'

'The terrible thing,' Sylvia said, crying on to my shoulder, 'is that I'm sure they would have made a wonderful couple.'

We pulled ourselves together slowly, weathering the headlines in the local newspaper, 'Local Doctor's Suicide', and the myriad questions it brought in its wake.

The summer days began to shorten, the surgeries were full as usual, and the children broke up from school. With no Robin to look after the practice a summer holiday was out of the question; besides I had no heart for it, neither had Sylvia. Miss Nisbet grew fatter and fatter and more and more apathetic; the paper work mounted and the patients suffered from my short temper. The sad summer turned quite suddenly to autumn and with the falling of the first leaves I came out of the trance I had lived through during the past few months.

One evening over dinner, I said to Sylvia, 'I have advertised for a new partner and a new secretary. We shall really have to let Miss Nisbet go,' I said, 'she can hardly get into her cubicle, poor thing.'

After many fruitless adverts and interviews I ended up with Dr Fouracre and Miss Simms, with neither of whom I could expect any romantic entanglements, although Sylvia did point out something to the effect that at night all the cats were grey. Miss Simms was grey to start with. She had been a medical secretary all her life but now felt the daily journey to town too much for her. On her first morning when she saw the chaos in poor Miss Nisbet's cubicle she nearly turned tail and walked out. I picked up a handful of letters idly, 'Oh, it's nothing at all, you'll soon get used to it; as I explained, it's a busy practice and I've been rather short of help lately.' I looked at her tightened lips and hazarded a guess that another pound a week might fix it. It did, and from that moment on Miss Simms became Queen of the May. She bossed, busy-bodied, and bustled; but in such an incredibly efficient way that I, at any rate, and seemingly the patients, were quite happy to bow to her will. Miss Nisbet faded out, if one could use such a term of one so huge, crying and tickled pink with Sylvia's gift of baby clothes.

In my advertisement for a new partner, not wishing to court more trouble, I stipulated a married man. Dr Fouracre was married and had two children.

'Incidentally,' he said on his first morning, 'why have you got such a "thing" about bachelors?'

I explained about Robin and he looked at me quizzically.

'To hell with the marriage lines,' he said, 'you must be aware that a man will give up profession and family, all his worldly goods in pursuit of a woman with whom he has a deeply satisfying experience.'

'You sound quite an expert on the subject.'

'I speak impersonally. I merely wanted to point out that married or bachelor a man is a man is a man...'

'I get the point.'

'I'm sorry about your partner. It must be difficult for you.'

'It was at first.' I held out my hand and said my Christian name. 'Miles,' he said, shaking it.

Sylvia brought in a tray. 'We shall celebrate what I hope will be many long years together with coffee and...' I inspected the tray, 'bourbon biscuits.'

'I would sell my soul for a bourbon biscuit,' he said, taking one and raising his coffee cup. 'Cheers!'

'Cheers!' I said, and trying to forget Robin, delved into my new engagement.

Miles Fouracre was an odd fish. Totally different to Robin, he had no patience for psychiatry of any description. He was extremely loath, and indeed considered it a mark of failure, to send any patient to hospital. He had just come back from three years' service in one of the under-developed countries and was used to doing anything from an appendix removal to an end to end anastomosis on the kitchen table.

'We had to do everything, my dear chap,' he said. 'I was the only medicine man for hundreds of miles. My God by the time I got them to the nearest hospital they would be not only dead but decomposed!'

I pointed out that this was London and the nearest hospital a matter of a mile and a half away.

'The Health Service has made sorting offices out of you,' he said, 'noses here, ears there, abdomens there…'

'All right,' I said, glad that Dr Fouracre was only on three months' trial, 'you be a one man band if you like; but I shall continue as usual.'

And a one man band he was. He lanced abscesses, removed cysts, and cauterised cervices with gay abandon. I had never before seen a medical practitioner who so enjoyed his work. Fortunately, since I was worried after their devotion to Robin, the patients adored him. He was a strange looking man, six foot three tall, burned black from tropical suns, and wearing a panama hat, indoors and out, in all weathers. He was kindness itself, though, and I did perhaps feel just a twinge of jealousy as Miss Simms allied herself with him on any point of controversy and gazed at him adoringly with the eyes of Theda Bara.

By the time the trees fully lost their leaves and stood silhouetted against the grey skies we had settled down again into routine. I relegated all thoughts of Robin to the back of my mind and was only reminded of him when a postcard arrived from Acapulco. 'It is so beautiful here, and empty. Lucy Gunner.' I gave it to Peter for the stamps, but the words remained in my head.

The day that was to beat all others for drama into that not uneventful year was a Thursday. I shall always remember it because Thursday was my half-day and we'd had tickets for Schwartzkopf at the Albert Hall. We had done the morning's visits which had been none too arduous and Miles had come back to the surgery so that we could check on anything there was for him to do that afternoon.

He was in his consulting-room and I was in mine. There was a lunch-time lull in the road and all that could be heard were the feet of the daily helps walking to the bus with their shopping bags.

Quite suddenly and totally unexpected there was a crash outside the house such as I had not heard since the Blitz, and that was a great many years ago. The whole house shook and the windows rattled.

Miles and I made for the waiting-room door and out into the street. One laundry van had collided at right angles with another laundry van. We saw the two drivers, apparently unhurt, and then to our horror that one of the vans had run over a woman whom presumably he had swerved to avoid. All that was visible were her legs and body sticking out from behind one of the wheels. The body was hugely pregnant.

'Come on, man,' Miles said, and appeared to fly down the steps and into the road.

I followed him. By the time we got to her the two drivers had too.

'Pick her up,' Miles said peremptorily, 'and bring her into the house, please.'

They were used to lugging heavy laundry boxes, but were trying to be gentle.

'There's no need to be careful,' Miles said, 'just hurry, every moment is vital!'

It was only then I saw what he meant when he said there was no need to be careful. The wheel had passed over the woman's head practically decapitating her. It wasn't a pretty sight. One of the van men started to grow green and tremble, the other one didn't look in too good a shape.

'I'll take her shoulders,' Miles said, 'grab her legs.'

Within moments, a trail of blood behind us, she was in my consulting-room and on the couch.

Miles pushed the laundry men and passers-by who had followed the little procession out on to the waiting-room steps and locked the door. In all my medical career I had not seen anything so horrible; the van had crushed the woman's skull to the thickness of a sheet of paper. All that remained were her limbs and a trunk with vastly swollen belly.

'She's dead, isn't she?' Miles said.

I thought he was being funny and said nothing.

'Do you certify this lady as dead? Feel her pulse, listen to her heart.'

I looked at her wondering what he was playing at.

'Yes. She's dead.'

'Right. Take her clothes off, quick as you can,' Miles said, and ran into his room.

Stupefied I started to unbutton her coat.

'For God's sake, man,' Miles said when he'd returned with his midwifery bag. He pushed me aside and with an enormous pair of scissors slit her garments from top to bottom.

When he had done this he pulled the couch away from the wall, and told me to go round the other side. Still wearing his panama hat he picked up a scalpel. 'Right,' he said, ignoring the knocking on the waiting-room door, 'let's go!'

It suddenly dawned. Miles Fouracre was going to attempt to perform a post-mortem Caesarean section. To rescue the baby even though the mother was dead. I now appreciated his hurry to get the baby out before the progressive anoxia to which it was being subjected inside the mother could cause irreversible damage.

To my never ending admiration Miles made a midline incision about six inches long, the upper third of which was above the umbilicus. He then opened the uterus through a longitudinal incision in the upper segment. After a few more moments' neat and utterly skilled work he ruptured the membranes and extracted the baby by grasping its lower limbs. Scarcely looking at it he handed the slippery child, which must have weighed at least ten pounds, to me and began to close the abdominal wounds. To my utter amazement the child began to cry lustily. I looked round for somewhere to put it, something to wrap it in. Finding nothing except some septic towels I raced into the kitchen where Sylvia was rolling pastry.

'What have you got there?' she said,

wrinkling her nose, 'and what on earth was that bang?'

'A baby! Quick take it, wrap it up, look after it.'

Afterwards I had to admit she was commonsense itself.

It took only a moment to sink in, then she wiped her hands on her pinafore, whipped open the drawer which held the clean tea-towels, and taking the baby from me wrapped it up.

'What do you want me to do with her? Bring her in?' she said, indicating the surgery.

'No! For God's sake don't come into there!'

There was an urgent ringing and knocking on the front door.

I gave Sylvia a push. 'Look take the baby upstairs and look after it. Whatever you do I don't want you to come down.'

She gave one backward glance at the pastry on the table and for once did as she was told.

In the surgery Miles had closed the wounds and covered the poor woman with a blanket off the couch. Sweat was pouring down his face. Bells and knocks and angry voices could be heard all round the house. Miles collapsed onto the chair.

'Okay,' he said. 'You can let them in.'

And in they came: police, neighbours,

reporters, and curious passers-by.

There was much licking of pencils as Miles told his almost unbelievable story.

'Where is it, if I may ask, sir?' the police officer finally said.

'What?'

'The baby.'

I called Sylvia and she came down with it whimpering in her arms.

'She's a little beauty,' Sylvia said. 'Just look at those deep blue eyes.' She handed the bundle to the officer who backed away.

'Look, er, I know it's rather awkward, madam, but if you could just hang on to the child for a half hour while we get in touch with the children's welfare officer ... the ambulance has already left you see.'

'As long as you like,' Sylvia said, 'she's gorgeous!'

The rest of the day passed like a dream. Poor Miles told his story a hundred times personally and over the telephone. He had his photo taken in a hundred poses always in the panama hat. He answered question after question. 'Yes, if the child is to survive there is a very slim time margin after the death of the mother.' 'No, he had never done a similar thing before.' 'Yes, there was a better chance of extracting a live child when the death of the mother is sudden.' 'Yes, he was sure that in this emergency he had taken the correct decision.'

Having squeezed the last drop of information out of us everyone went away. We
cleaned up the surgery and Miles went
home for lunch.

We decided to open the door, whose bell
rang all afternoon, to none but the police.
To reporters, who had quickly got hold of
the story from their colleagues, we said
there was nothing to report.

We admitted the Children's Welfare Officer
who came to take the baby to a Home until
enquiries could be made about its relatives.

To my surprise, Sylvia said: 'Oh, please
couldn't I keep her? Just until you find her
family, I mean.'

Having assured herself of Sylvia's compet-
ence to look after the child the Welfare
Officer agreed, saying she would get in
touch with us as soon as possible, and had
we any dried milk?

Sylvia tucked the baby up in a drawer
under my watchful and weary-with-shock
eye, while she nipped out for bottles, nap-
pies, shawls, and nappy pins. Out of the
parcel which she bought home also fell vests,
nightees, bootees, matinée jackets, and a
rattle.

'We're not going to need all that for a
couple of days,' I said.

'I have a feeling,' Sylvia said, kissing the
baby on its soft head, 'that it will be longer
than that. I shall call her Eugénie.' Our eyes

met. I recalled a voice from long ago 'there will be others, little ones' and went to rescue Napoleon from his solitary confinement in my certificate drawer.

The feelings inside Sylvia proved to be right. The poor woman who had been run over had neither husband nor relatives. The baby would have to go to a foster home.

'She already has one; Penny and Peter would be broken-hearted to lose her,' Sylvia said, gazing at her latest daughter. 'Then perhaps later we can adopt her officially.'

'There seems no reason why not,' the Welfare Officer said, 'no reason at all.' She smiled at Napoleon's black and white face keeping guard at the end of the makeshift cot. 'I see she already has a friend.'

And that is how by the time we saw the old year out, there were tears in our eyes for Robin, poor Robin who had died for love, and laughter in our hearts for so much that had happened in the past twelve months, and happiness for the year that had ended small as it had begun with our princess Eugénie.

The publishers hope that this book has given you enjoyable reading. Large Print Books are especially designed to be as easy to see and hold as possible. If you wish a complete list of our books please ask at your local library or write directly to:

Dales Large Print Books
Magna House, Long Preston,
Skipton, North Yorkshire.
BD23 4ND

This Large Print Book, for people
who cannot read normal print,
is published under the auspices of

THE ULVERSCROFT FOUNDATION